A Lighthouse of Ocean and Fog

Nellie Brooks

Merpaper Press LLC

Edited by Karen Meeus Editing

Published by Merpaper Press LLC

CONTENTS

CHAPTER 1

The afternoon sun was still bright when Jenny switched off the ancient TV that stood in her living room. "Now we've seen it, girls. It's over. We can relax." She yawned and stretched as if the movie had locked her joints.

Billie blinked and looked around, letting her gaze wander outside. The late-summer sun glittered on the ocean, and a line of majestic pelicans drifted across the water of the forgotten cove, their wings motionless as the sea breeze carried them past the beach and the historic mansion that had once been a hotel.

Jenny curled up again on her couch. "So. What did you think of the movie, Billie?"

"Dunno," Billie said unhelpfully.

In fact, she knew very well.

She didn't like the movie. She did not like what she had just watched.

But before telling them exactly what she didn't like about the handiwork of her movie-directing ex-husband, she wanted her friends' unbiased opinions.

Sort of.

Billie eyed the lot of them, strewn across sofas and chairs as they were.

Really—if she was being honest—she wanted them to agree with her.

Because Jenny, Faye, and Ava knew how Ian had treated her. He'd cheated and lied, even pulling their two boys into his deception when they were still only babies and too young to realize what was happening.

When Billie finally caught on and called Ian out, he admitted everything.

Everything was called Francesca, had large, dark doe-eyes and a skinny waist, and was just another young actress falling for Ian's artistic bit.

Billie frowned.

Ian hadn't even been famous back then.

Now he was.

Stupid movie.

Ava popped the last cheese cube on the charcuterie tray into her mouth. "The film wasn't all bad, though, was it?" Chewing thoughtfully, she smoothed her blue skirt over her knees.

Billie groaned. "Please don't call it a *film*." Their divorce was decades old, but Ian's intellectual pretensions still got on her nerves. "It's a movie. The word is good enough."

Outside on the beach, the sea lion Polly barked, and a sleek young male that had been sticking close to her for the last two weeks barked back.

"Ava's right, Bills. It wasn't entirely bad." Faye shifted her modest baby bump to get more comfortable. "I watched all the way through, and I don't do that for many movies. If I get bored, that's it for me. I walk away."

"You didn't walk away," Jenny agreed and fluffed a pillow.

"Did you notice that the wife *dies* at the end?" Billie protested. Could they not see what Ian had done there?

"I did notice that," Ava admitted. "And I have to say, that was a gratuitous death. She could have easily walked away from that car accident and started a new life herself. The judge already gave him the house and the kids, so what did it matter whether she lived or died?"

"And a new woman," Billie added sourly. "He got the house, the kids, and the beautiful woman who wasn't his wife."

"To be fair, the wife was already dead when he re-married," Faye said soothingly.

"Exactly. The only reason she died was to make him look better. Pfft. Give me a break." Billie wasn't fooled. "Nothing else in the story demanded she'd die. There was no plot advancement. It was just to make his do-over look nice and clean."

"And when you say *his*—do you mean the character or your ex?" Faye asked.

Good question.

Billie drained the last of the wine from the bottle into her glass while she considered her answer. "My ex-husband," she then announced. "Clearly, the character was based on him."

"Nah," Jenny said vaguely.

"You never met him," Billie pointed out. "The actor even wore Ian's old glasses. I swear."

"No, he did not, Bills," Faye said. "I knew Ian well enough. His glasses were a bit different."

What? Why was Faye not having her back? The glasses were *exactly* the same.

"I need more wine." Billie rose and picked up the green bottle that stood on the delicate side table, holding it up to the light. "This is so empty." Disgruntled, she left the living room, making her way to the kitchen.

The hotel had been built by one of the town's founders for his aging mother, who immediately left again to move into a village cottage with her friends. Jenny's grandparents snapped up the abandoned mansion for a song and a dance and converted it into a hotel, where they put up paying and non-paying guests alike.

In the hotel's heyday in the sixties and seventies, everyone had been welcome to stay. Especially single mothers—since Jenny's mom, Willow, was one of them. Grandma Rosie gave the young women a home and a family when they needed it most and let them stay as long as they needed. The end of the hotel's glory came when Willow got lost in the wilderness of the coastal redwood forest and died.

Grief-stricken, Grandma Rosie closed the hotel and sent Willow's daughter, Jenny, and Willow's sister, Georgie, across the country for a new beginning in beautiful Nantucket.

"*Another* bottle?" Faye remarked dryly when Billie returned, wine in hand. "You guys have been glugging away all evening. How are you not drunk?"

"Don't be jealous, Faye," said Ava. "Once you've had your baby and spent a year or so nursing, you'll get a sip." Ava patted Faye's shoulder. "But I'm happy to bring you another seltzer. What flavor do you want?"

Mollified by the offer, Faye patted her baby bump. "Thank you, Ava. But I've had so much water, I already feel like I'm mostly bladder."

"Eww, Faye. Thanks for putting that picture in my mind." Shaking her head, Billie set down the bottle and went back to the kitchen to refill their charcuterie tray. The rich meats and cheeses countered the alcohol.

Because Faye was right, Billie had drunk too much. Billie's brother, Jon, was an excellent vintner who had generously supplied the wine for the evening.

Even though he not only was Billie's brother but also dated Jenny, he'd excused himself from watching the movie. His excuses were threadbare at best, but he was a peaceful, grounded person who didn't like to be around when the topic turned to Ian.

Because Jon knew that Billie, after all these years, was still angry.

Right after the divorce, there'd been months of good progress. Billie had worked through tears and pain and self-doubt. Friends and family and a good therapist helped her process Ian's betrayal and the sudden change in her circumstances.

But eventually, Billie had hit a wall that was as solid as granite.

Nothing she did chipped the stone, let alone shifted it.

Tired of musing and licking her wounds, she had finally lied to her therapist, Klara, claiming she was no longer mad at her treacherous ex. Klara was kind and smart, and she didn't believe Billie for a second. Billie knew it was the too-high pitch of voice and her shifting eyes that gave her away. But either way, she stopped scheduling sessions, and after a while, Klara stopped calling to find out why.

Like the embers of a forest fire still smoldering under green moss long after the rain, Billie's anger at Ian simmered. She was embarrassed at harboring any feelings for him at all anymore. But granite is hard and embers smolder, and Billie couldn't change a thing about it.

Most of the time, she tried hard not to think about Ian. But the memories came back to her every time she saw her younger son. Louis had inherited his dad's good looks. And once in a while, Billie and Ian had to talk on the phone about something that concerned the boys. They kept it short and civil. But afterward, Billie always dreamed she walked along a dark street. Barefoot, ugly, and alone.

With a sigh, she now set down the empty charcuterie tray on the kitchen counter. Then she started to pull wax-paper-wrapped packages and foil-covered goodies from the fridge.

Soon, the kitchen island was strewn with snack foods. Plates with cubed cheeses and salami, sweet and savory pies, bowls with chips and dips, platters with crisp emerald grapes, ruby-red strawberries, and golden-white peaches waited their turn to return to the fridge.

Billie took a moment to gather herself.

At least they had come to hold her hand through watching the movie. Rallying around Billie, the girls had organized a camp-out at the hotel so they could wait together for Ian's movie to air. Billie was grateful. Annoyingly, the movie had won a critical award. For weeks, the small town of Mendocino Cove had been littered with flyers and posters, giddily announcing the cinematic triumph of their former inhabitant.

But the public's opinion was still out. And that was what counted, wasn't it?

Yes.

Yes, of course it was.

Billie put the things back into the fridge and picked up the heavy wooden board. Balancing olives and strawberries and cheese cubes, she made her way back into the airy living room where the sea breeze played with the long, sheer curtains in front of the open French doors.

It was beautiful. Billie exhaled, her breath leaving at the pace of the graceful dance.

She and her friends had lovely lives, full of swaying curtains and kind brothers and delicious cheeses.

Billie had so much. She had so much more than most—more than enough, certainly.

Then why couldn't she let Ian be? Why not simply let go of whatever blows he'd dealt her heart?

Billie wanted to pour seawater on the smoldering embers of her anger to see them flicker and die. She wanted to crack the granite of her wrath like the gulls in the cove cracked mussels and sea urchins with their sturdy beaks.

Maybe it was because Billie had loved Ian. He was the father of her sons. The wound he had dealt was too deep, the poison of his betrayal too corrosive. No matter how terribly much Billie wanted to heal, she could not figure out how to let go of the last memories nor the last regrets for the life they had promised each other at the altar.

"Okay, girls." Billie set the charcuterie board on the sofa table and put her hands on her hips. "Time to be honest. Get it out."

"Get what out?" Faye asked cautiously.

Billie loved Faye—but right now, her friend had a shifty look in her eyes. Billie narrowed her own. "Admit that the movie wasn't that good."

The words flowed together in one long whine.

Themoviewasnthatgooood.

Billie snapped her lips shut and looked from one friend to the next.

Faye slouched on the sofa, mouth half-closed and not admitting anything. Ava stood by the fireplace, one hand on the mantel like some old duke contemplating life. Jenny had gone to stand in the open door, admiring the beach and letting the light wind tousle her shoulder-length blonde hair and tug on her yellow sundress.

Billie dropped her arms. "Guys? Ladies? Little help?"

It was outrageous.

She was there at the drop of a coin when they needed her, and the *one* time she—

Jenny turned around. "It wasn't perfect," she said mildly. "The wife didn't need to die. But it wasn't terrible either, Billie. There was a story with a beginning and an end, and there were characters with hopes and dreams and fears. Don't count on Ian's fame going away quite yet."

"Plus, the movie had a couple of good plot twists. People like twists," Faye added.

"I agree." Ava let go of the fireplace mantle. "Brace yourself, Billie. It might get worse before it gets better."

"Aww, come on, you traitors. I don't have to *brace* myself." Billie stabbed the wine bottle's cork with a corkscrew and yanked it out, then poured herself a generous glass.

The cool, red wine was light and dry, and it reminded her of her brother's beautiful vineyard with its sweetly rolling hills and gorgeous views. Even better, it reminded her of the large family she had in Mendocino Cove.

"I don't have to brace myself," Billie repeated stubbornly. And then, out of the pettiness of her heart, she added, "Not that I care one way or the other."

"It's okay if you do care." Faye shifted her baby bump into a more comfortable position. "We understand."

Then why didn't they back her up? Billie would have done it for them in a heartbeat. No matter how good or bad the movie was, she'd have wanted them to feel better. And Billie wasn't just being vindictive, either. The movie truly wasn't that good. A plot wasn't enough; it also had to be interesting. And characters with hopes and dreams were only a start; they also needed to stand up for themselves and *do* something to fulfill them.

Other than offing their wives.

"As far as I know, I am the only wife Ian's ever had." Billie took another sip.

"Still doesn't mean the wife in the movie was based on you," Faye pointed out.

"I agree." Jenny came and started to clear plates and glasses off the coffee table. "From what little you told me about your ex, Billie, he seems to be smart enough. Even if he was no good."

"I don't know about smart," Billie muttered half-heartedly.

Jenny continued as if Billie hadn't said anything at all. "He's too smart to base his movie wife on you. Or any real person. He knows better than that."

"The movie wife had brown, short, curly hair like me," Billie muttered and emptied her glass. "The only difference between the two of us is that I didn't lose my life in a car crash."

"There are other differences too," Ava said. "Like, the movie wife was desperate, and you are obviously not. You have a happy life. You're the most independent, the strongest woman I know, Billie." She picked up a bowl of glazed almonds and studied them absent-mindedly, then set the bowl back down. "How about we stop snacking and go for a short walk on the bluff? Air out and forget about the movie. It was nothing special, Billie. It will be on TV for a while, but there's no reason for you to watch it again."

"Does nobody want a slice of the good salami?" Billie asked helplessly. "I just put more on the tray."

"I'm stuffed to the gills." Arms full of used dishes, Jenny left for the kitchen.

"Fine." Billie picked up her untouched tray and carried it back.

"If we want to take a walk, we should leave now." Jenny looked up from lowering glasses into the sudsy water in the sink. "Jon is coming soon to pick you up, isn't he?"

Billie nodded.

"Faye?"

"What, Jenny?" Faye appeared in the door, more plates in her hands.

"Are you staying the night here, or are you going home?"

Faye was four months pregnant, hadn't had a sip of wine, and was very capable of driving herself. "Gabe is going to pick me up when Jon comes for Billie."

Jenny smiled and shook her head. "He spoils you."

Faye sighed and put her hands on her belly. She was still struggling with morning sickness—and the concept of becoming a mother. "Believe me when I say I deserve it."

"Of course you do," Jenny confirmed and dried her hands.

Billie crossed her arms. "On second thought, it's too late to walk," she claimed. "Jon's going to be here any minute."

He'd be early for a chance to catch a moment with Jenny, not to save his grumpy sister. Billie knew that. Right now, she didn't appreciate it. This had been a mistake. She wanted to be home, in her cozy cottage, alone.

"Billie. Baby. Don't be mad. We love you." Faye hugged her from the back.

"I'm not mad." Billie exhaled loudly. "I just want you guys to have my back. I need it."

"We do. We have your back," Jenny promised. "Don't worry. The movie doesn't matter. You don't need us to lie to have your back."

"In this case, I do."

"When it really counts, we'll say what you want to hear. Oh, listen. Is that Jon?" Jenny craned her neck to look out of the window. But the window went out the side, and there was only a cypress tree and a rhododendron bush so old and confused it bloomed all year long. Still, Jenny seemed to get whatever information she was looking for. "Yes, it's Jon! I'll go let him in."

"Is Gabe with him?" Faye asked, just as excited as Jenny.

They rushed out the door, leaving Billie alone.

The voices coming from the lobby told her that Jon, Gabe, and even Ava's husband, Bruno, had arrived and were cheerfully greeted by their loving partners.

"I'm an independent woman with grown children and a sufficient income," Billie whispered to herself. "I don't need nobody." Slowly, she lowered her hands into the sudsy water and started to do the washing up Jenny had abandoned.

All the world was in love. Only she was alone. No, worse. She was alone, and her ex was rubbing his triumph in her face.

Billie had never felt this lonely.

Her cell phone buzzed. Irritated at the timing, Billie shook off the bubbles. Her animal rescue station had stood empty for weeks. A rescue call was long overdue. Surely a pelican had broken a claw, or a sea lion pup lost its way.

Walking through the living room and onto the patio, Billie answered the phone without bothering to first check the screen. "Yeah. Who's this?"

CHAPTER 2

B illie? It's me. It's Ian."

"Ian?" Heat shot into Billie's face. The thought skittered through her mind that he knew she'd been thinking about him. But that was impossible.

She took a breath. "What's up?"

"I was wondering... Did you see *I, Liberation?* My movie that received the Cinemania award?"

"Uh." Billie sighed the breath out again. "Yeah. I did see it. Just now. Hot off the press, huh?" Surely, he couldn't be so vain to expect his ex-wife to *enjoy* the movie he'd made about a man liberating himself from the yoke of his marriage.

Ian waited for a beat to let her praise his directing skills. When she didn't say anything, he laugh-coughed. "Hey, that's all right. I'm glad you at least watched it. But that's not why I called."

Billie tucked her chin in. "No?"

"No. I wanted to discuss something else with you, Billie."

"What's that?"

"In a nutshell? I want to come back to Mendocino Cove."

"You want to—why?" That was the last thing she needed.

It took a while before he answered. "I used to live there, Billie. I love the town. It's where I grew up. It's where I ran across the bluffs as a child."

"Ian, you grew up in Hanover," Billie reminded him. "You only moved here after we got married. It was *me* who ran across the bluffs."

"I remember fishing in the rock pools. Once, I caught a baby flounder. I still remember the feeling of it in my hand." His voice had a dreamlike quality.

"*I* caught the flounder. I told you how it felt. Ian, you are from Hanover. There are no rock pools there."

"Hmm. Maybe it was you. It doesn't matter. I *feel* like it was me. You know me—I'm a dreamer."

"Okay. All right." Billie knew what he was doing.

Hanover was nice enough. It was a bigger town an hour inland from the coast, where there was space for a mall and a mega mart, a handful of supermarkets, restaurant strips, fast-food places, coffee chains. The people from Mendocino Cove went shopping for affordable garden sets and reduced appliances in Hanover but otherwise rarely saw a reason to go that far.

Still, it was a good, robust town full of air conditioners and automated doors and paved streets as black and shiny as wet seals.

But it was a town without a coast, without romance, and without any ambition other than to keep its citizens in fine fettle.

More than anything, Ian was ambitious and driven. He meant to live an extraordinary life and, more than once, he'd told Billie he was determined to leave behind his undistinguished past. Back then, Billie still nodded and tried to understand her husband. Until she discovered that she, too, was part of the undistinguished past he meant to leave behind.

Unlike Hanover, Mendocino Cove was a beautiful town. It wasn't rich, and there was barely a street that was paved black as a wet seal. Mostly, the asphalt was bleached from the sun and cracked from old age. Many shops couldn't afford air conditioning, and some people didn't even *like* fast food. But they were good neighbors who knew each other's names, the school was one of the best on the coast, and there was a picturesque romance to growing up between wildflower-bedazzled bluffs, private coves, and sandy beaches.

Billie knew how lucky she was and never minded sharing her scenic hometown. But Ian claiming her childhood memories as his own was too much.

It was *her* flounder memory.

"I *practically* grew up in Mendocino Cove," he insisted, oblivious. When Billie inhaled to answer, he coughed again, cutting her off.

"Are you sick?" she asked, irritated.

"No, don't worry. I was just saying that I'm on my way to Mendocino Cove. And I'd like to see you, if you don't mind. We haven't met up in too long."

Now it was Billie who didn't know what to say. Not once, in all their years apart, had Ian asked to see her.

"Why?" she asked finally.

"I just would like to," he replied. "Why not? We used to be married, after all. Remember?"

Billie shook her head, knowing full well he couldn't see it. "I don't think that's such a good idea." She noticed the softening of her voice and nervously moistened her lips.

Was she, like Ava, unaware that she was still in love with her husband?

No. For one, Ian wasn't her husband. Two, Billie had fallen out of love hard and fast and in a very real way when she found out about Francesca.

"I just think it'd be nice to catch up," Ian said. "Maybe we should have a glass of wine at your brother's winery?"

"How do you even know Jon has a winery?" Billie asked before she could stop herself.

"The boys told me. They like what he's done with the property. I'd sure love to see his tasting room and everything."

"I don't want to meet at Jon's," Billie started, but then she deflated.

Did she really not want to talk? He'd already said he wanted to come to Mendocino Cove. She couldn't stop him. Of course he would do what he wanted.

What then?

Maybe sitting down over a glass of wine with him was exactly what Billie needed.

It was the only thing she hadn't tried yet.

Maybe sitting down and talking like two mature adults was exactly what she *wanted.*

Billie felt her knee-jerk resistance soften. "Okay. When do you want to meet?"

"How about in an hour? I'm on my way now. I'm almost over the mountain range."

Billie sat on the closest of the wicker patio chairs. So soon?

She checked the time.

It was only five, and she had no plans for the evening. Her friends were either busy kissing their men, or they were the kissed men themselves. Only she had nothing to do. She didn't even have any rescue animals to care for.

There was definitely time to hang out with her ex.

"Okay," Billie conceded. "Jon's closed today." Not true, but she could do without her brother watching them the entire time.

A gull screamed, and she looked up.

"How about your place? The cottage? The boys say it is beautiful with all the flowers."

For years, Ian never asked for as much as a phone call, and now he wanted to come to her cottage?

"I don't know," she hedged. "The Mermaid Galley would be better. We can have a glass of wine and maybe dinner. Have you eaten yet?"

"No, no time with all this award craziness." Ian inhaled happily. "I lost ten pounds and ten ounces. Can you imagine? *Ten* ounces. Ha!"

Cinemania happened over a month ago. Billie was embarrassed to know the date; she had followed Ian's story too closely. Yet it didn't seem likely that things were still so crazy he couldn't snatch a bite to eat. Then again, Billie wasn't an acclaimed director and didn't know how these things worked. Who was she to say?

Wine and dinner, then. Maybe he'd say he'd never gotten over her, and then she could ask about the dead wife in *I, Liberation*.

"So I'll see you in an hour at the Galley," she concluded.

"Perfect. I can't wait, Billie." Ian hung up.

Billie's hand holding the phone dropped to her side. Then she stood, running a hand through her hair.

There was only an hour to prepare. The drive from the hotel to her cottage took a few minutes. She definitely needed a shower. She could wear the new blue shorts and a white blouse, maybe the blue wedge sandals, since they wouldn't take a walk. No—dinner and wine. Not *shorts*. A dress. Not to impress, of course not. It was only normal to want to look nice when going out, no matter with whom. People were bound to recognize Ian and stop to talk about the movie.

Something rapped sharply behind Billie, startling her.

Jenny stood, knuckle on the French door, smiling at Billie. "Hey."

"Hey." Billie held up the phone. "I had to take a call."

"Everything okay? Your cheeks are flushed. Who was it?"

That was the thing with friends. They asked questions and wanted answers. Then they had opinions.

Billie scratched her chin. "Um. Ian?"

"The man of the hour himself? Why did he call?" Eyeing her curiously, Jenny stepped out of the living room onto the patio.

"He wanted to know how I liked his movie."

"Seriously? What did you say?" Wide-eyed, Faye joined Jenny at the door. She'd clearly caught their last words.

"I can't remember."

"You can't remember?" Ava stepped outside as well and took one of the comfortable wicker chairs. "You must remember *something*."

Billie sighed and lifted her hands in defeat. "Look. My brain's scrambled eggs right now. He wants to meet in an hour at the Mermaid Galley and talk about coming back to town. I'm in shock, but I should probably go and see what he wants."

"Oh, wow." Faye's eyes widened even more. "He calls to ask you on a date the night of his movie's big airing? I mean, he could meet up with literally *anyone* tonight."

Billie looked up. Of her three best friends in the world, Faye knew the most about her. They had both stayed in Mendocino Cove when Jenny moved to Nantucket and Ava to Seattle.

Since they had come back home, the four of them saw each other almost daily. They never ran out of things to say to catch each other up about the past.

But Faye had been there every step of the way with Billie.

Faye had witnessed Ian asking Billie out for the first time, the night of the sea-glass festival. Billie, breathless and red-cheeked with youth and happiness, had reported their first kiss to Faye. Faye had been the best maid at the wedding. She'd held Billie's still-long hair when Billie threw up. At first, because of the pregnancies. Later, when Ian admitted his affair with Francesca.

"I know," Billie murmured, her eyes locked with Faye's.

Faye shook her head once. "What are you going to wear?"

Billie checked her phone for the time. "This, if Jon doesn't show up soon."

"Jon's already here," Jenny reminded her. "He's having a quick bite to eat. He's been working in the vineyard all day."

"Let's go," Billie murmured. "Jon can eat at my house while I change."

"But you and Ian meeting doesn't mean anything, does it?" Faye tilted her head.

Billie took a deep breath. "It doesn't mean anything," she confirmed. "Of course not. Of course it doesn't mean anything. He probably just wants to brag about his movie."

"Uh-oh." Faye sighed. "Why don't I believe you?"

CHAPTER 3

Y ou are really going out with Ian? Are you sure you want that?" Jon glanced at Billie. They stood parked in front of her cottage, but neither one of them made an attempt to get out of the truck.

"Worst-case scenario, he wants to brag," Billie repeated what she'd told the girls. "But Jon—there is something important he wants to talk about. I can tell."

Jon's eyes searched her face. "Does he want to get back together?"

Billie shook her head. But in the deepest depth of her heart, she nodded. "Why would he?" she asked, her voice too light.

"Why *wouldn't* he?" Jon asked. "He asked to marry you once already. You're a wonderful person, Billie. You are compassionate, kind, and you're fun."

Billie's cheeks flushed warmly. It wasn't every day that her older brother complimented her. "Thanks, Jon," she murmured.

"No, listen to me," he said as if she hadn't heard him. "Don't let him chat you up. People don't change. He's ancient history, isn't he?"

"Sure. Ancient history." Billie nodded. The sun was dipping toward the ocean. She had only half an hour left to get ready for dinner. Tops.

"Hmm." Jon sighed. "Well, off you go. Don't buy whatever he's trying to sell, hear me?"

"Loud and clear." Billie opened the door and jumped to the ground. "Thanks for the ride."

To her surprise, Jon opened his door and got out as well.

"What are you doing?" she asked. "Don't you want to get back to Jenny?"

"I've changed my mind." He closed the door and started walking toward the cottage. "I'm driving you to the Mermaid Galley. You've had too much wine to drive yourself."

"I've had a ton of snacks. In an hour, I'll be all right." Billie hurried to keep up with her brother's long strides.

"Frankly, if you were sober, I don't think you would even consider meeting Ian at a restaurant," Jon remarked dryly. "Instead you're making gooey eyes." He stopped in front of the cottage door and pulled out his own set of keys.

Billie held the stitch in the left side of her waist. "Hff."

"And now you're out of breath. You're only out of breath when you drink."

"Okay." Billie tried to pant quieter. "Thanks for offering to drive me, I guess. But you're not coming inside the Galley for dinner."

"No, I'm going to drop you off and run." Jon held the door for her, and Billie entered the cottage. "Unlike you, I have no desire to see your ex again."

"That's... Yeah. I understand." Until a few minutes ago, that had been Billie's prevailing feeling as well. "But it's been so long ago, Jon. You're not still holding a grudge, are you?"

"Now I'm *really* concerned about how drunk you are," he murmured and closed the front door. "Are you sure you wouldn't rather have some nice, cool water and go to bed?"

"Ha-ha. No. There's a bacon quiche in the kitchen if you're still hungry." Billie turned and headed for the upstairs bedroom. It was too late for a shower, but she at least wanted to wash her face and put on makeup.

It took her more time than she had to get ready. She picked out her dress of pearl-gray linen so fine it shimmered in the moonlight, but it was wrinkled, and she had to give it a quick steam. When it was smooth, she slipped into it, stepped into the black strappy sandals she never got to wear, put on lipstick, and wet her hands to knead her curls into a more conventional shape.

What if the dinner went well? What if, at the end of it, Ian asked to do something tomorrow too? She'd probably say no. She still didn't like him, after all. He'd be just as conceited as always. And Billie didn't want to have to invite him here or to the winery. But she shouldn't be impolite, either.

Quickly, she browsed on her phone for local events and on an impulse booked two tickets for a tour of the lighthouse on Mendocino Island. She'd had no idea the town reopened it, but it would be great to see it. A short ferry ride, a walk, the tour... It would take sixty minutes, all of it in full view of the public.

When she came back down, Jon whistled. "You clean up nice. Ian will eat his heart out when he sees you."

"I hope not," Billie said, trying not to show how much Jon's words pleased her. The petty urge of making an ex—no matter how long it had been—regret their rejection was too hard to resist.

"Come on then, beautiful." Jon opened the door and held it open, then picked a sprig of lavender and handed it to her. "In lieu of the bouquet he isn't going to bring."

Billie took it. "Um. Thanks, I guess. You're being very sweet. But I don't expect flowers from Ian."

"That's the problem."

They drove the short distance to the Mermaid Galley in silence.

Their friend Michael ran the small restaurant on the main street, and tonight, Hannah was working here too. Hannah had her own successful catering business and split her time between keeping Michael company at the Mermaid Galley and the winery. Every other day, she served dinner there out of her converted food truck.

"Thanks, Jon," Billie said when her brother pulled up at the curb.

"Call me when you want me to pick you up."

"Will do." Billie got out and waved, then closed the door.

Her brother waved back, made the universal sign for calling him on the phone, and then he left.

Billie looked up at the Mermaid Galley. The restaurant faced the sea, and the fiery reds and burned golds of the sinking sun painted it in magical colors.

Sometimes, magic happened to the most mundane, average things. People, too.

Billie held a hand to her forehead. "What are you doing?" she murmured to herself on the empty street. "Are you *excited* to see him?"

Twenty years, they'd been divorced, and mostly, she'd been angry at him. But now, her heartbeat told a different story. One she hadn't realized still existed.

Billie let her hand slip from her forehead to her heart, pressing against it, hard. "Quiet, stupid," she murmured. "Ian's no good for us."

Maybe that was the reason her wall of anger didn't come down. She'd tackled it the wrong way, fighting her disappointment and sense of betrayal, when really, she should have fought the last flames of her love for him.

Was he planning on rekindling those embers now?

Gooseflesh crawled over Billie's arms, and she rubbed them.

Then she reached for the wooden door and pushed, entering the Galley before she could think better of it.

"Hi, Billie." Hannah had already spotted her. "You look nice. What brings you over here? I thought you guys were meeting up to watch the liberation thing?" She tossed her carefully tended dreadlocks over her shoulder and smiled at Billie.

"Hi, Hannah." Billie went to the table where Hannah sat, writing something into a ledger. "We did watch it, but it's over. I'm meeting someone else tonight."

"There's a single guy upstairs." Hannah pushed back her chair and stood. "I came downstairs to give myself a break from staring at him. I couldn't help it."

"Good-looking, huh?"

"Very. You're a lucky gal."

"Don't be so sure. He's my ex." Billie pushed her shoulder strap higher. "The father of my sons."

"Oh shoot, is he really?" Hannah's eyes widened. "I had no idea. The big director himself, here to see you?"

Billie looked around. "Where's Michael?"

"He's cooking up a new dish. He's not going to come out of the kitchen all evening." Hannah shook her head but smiled a secret little smile.

Either she liked the new dish, or Michael had finally kissed her in the kitchen. The entire town was waiting with bated breath for Michael to make his move.

Billie smiled back. "That might be for the best. I don't think he'll like Ian." She glanced at the staircase leading upstairs. There would be a fantastic view of the ocean once the moon rose over the water.

"Go ahead." Hannah gathered her ledger and pens. "I'll bring you a drink in a moment."

"What's he having?"

"A Shanghai Skipper."

"Is he really? What is that?"

"Don't know." Hannah grinned. "No one's ever or-dered one before. I just poured random stuff together. He seems okay with it."

"Then he doesn't know what it is, either." Billie shook her head. "I'll just have lemon seltzer water, Hannah. The movie earlier this evening came with a lot of wine. I've had enough for the night."

"Very wise. Hey, if you guys aren't too long, I can drive you home." Hannah checked her watch.

"Thanks. I'll see how it goes up there." Billie smiled again, and then she climbed the stairs.

Like Hannah had predicted, Ian was the only patron in the upstairs dining room. He was sitting with his back to the stairs, seemingly lost in the beauty of the sunset.

"Ian?" Billie tugged a curl in place.

He turned, smiling when he saw her. "Billie! It's so good to see you." His chair scraped over the tiles as he stood. "Will you join me?"

"Yes." Billie weaved her way through the tables and pulled out a chair for herself. "How are you?" She sat, hanging her purse over the back rest.

"Good. Excellent." Ian sat as well. His Shanghai Skip-per concoction had a tiny purple paper umbrella in it, which made Billie smile.

Hannah arrived with the requested glass of bubbling water.

"Can I order appetizers?" Ian asked.

"Do you want the card?"

"No—just a sampler for two, please."

"Sure thing." Hannah left again.

Ian rested his elbows on the table and folded his hands. The look in his eyes was earnest. "It's so good to see you, Billie. You look fantastic. It's been too long—I mean, really. It's been too long."

"Hmm. It has been a few years, hasn't it?" She tugged her dress in place. "You look good too, Ian. Um. Congratulations on the movie. I didn't like it, but I hear the critics do."

For a fraction of a second, Ian looked pained. Then he rallied and even laughed quietly. "You always were straightforward." He leaned back. "And I always adored that about you."

"That's news to me." She smiled back. "I could've sworn it wasn't one of the qualities you enjoyed."

His eyes wandered to her chest. Billie was curvy, and she knew for a fact he had enjoyed *that* quality of hers. It was the one thing she and Francesca had in common.

Billie shifted to escape his eyes. Hannah arrived with a platter of mini crab cakes, crostini, barbecue kebabs, and scallop ceviche bites that she set between them.

"Anything else I can get you?" Hannah looked at Billie.

Billie nodded that she was okay. "We're good for now. Thank you."

"Alrighty. Let me know." Hannah nodded back and left, disappearing into the upstairs kitchen instead of back downstairs.

Ian took a crab cake and put it on his plate. "So, Billie. There's a reason I asked you to have dinner with me. I hope you'll hear me out."

Billie looked up at the formal words. "What is it?" She took her glass and sipped the water.

Ian bit into his cake, then wiped his hands on a paper napkin. Outside, the moon was rising into a velvety plum sky.

"I'm not just visiting. I want to move back here for good." He put down his napkin.

"You want to *move* back," Billie repeated. "Not *come* back, move back."

"Yes. To Mendocino Cove."

"Move here *permanently?*" The words settled uncomfortably in her brain.

"Yes. Billie, it's my hometown. I used to live here, remember?" He leaned forward and winked. "I'm not asking your permission, darling, because I don't need it. I'm telling you."

Almost, Billie snapped not to call her darling.

Dinner and a conversation were one thing. Having Ian move back into her hometown was another.

She leaned back and relaxed her shoulders, aware that he was watching closely.

Faye's ex, Lex, had moved back into town after long years away. Faye, too, had been apprehensive, but it was working just fine. Better than fine, in fact. The two were friends again. Mingling in the same social group was no longer a problem.

Ava and her husband had even renewed their vows in a beautiful ceremony.

Maybe there was love and forgiveness in the water coming from the taps of Mendocino Cove.

Billie forced a smile back on her lips. "Of course you don't need my permission. I know that."

"But I *did* want to let you know. And I *do* want your permission, if you can find it in your heart." Ian put his arm on the table, the open hand an invitation for her.

Slowly, she laid hers in it. His fingers closed over hers, and his thumb started to rub the back of her hand.

Billie tilted her head back as warmth started to spread up her arm. "You have my permission, Ian. For what it's worth." Luckily, the only house close to her own cottage that was for sale was already being bought by Christy, a friend of Billie's neighbor, Agatha Simon.

"I have my eye on a little place," Ian admitted as if he knew where her thoughts had strayed. "Seaview Lane."

"Seaview Lane? Wow." A little outside the old village, the lane was as swanky as Mendocino Cove got. Certainly, the modern coastal houses in the private community were priced in the millions. None of them were adequately described as *little places*.

"Yes. The negotiations are going on right now."

"Well." Billie pulled her hand back. Under the table, she rubbed it on her dress to get rid of the scalding trail his rubbing thumb had left on her sensitive skin. "Good luck to you."

"It'll be good for the boys." He smiled. "Now they can visit us both in one trip. Don't you think so?"

"Sure. They're busy people." Their sons, Ben and Louis, had a hard time getting out of their many commitments. It would make their lives easier not having to drive down to LA to see their dad. And who knew? Maybe having Ian close by would be good for Billie too, if it tempted the boys to drive over more often.

"There's something else." Ian drew back his empty hand and cleared his throat.

"What?" Billie looked up.

"Billie—I'm getting married."

She blinked. "Married?"

"Yes. I'm getting married again. Even though it's been years since our divorce, I thought you'd like to know that too."

Billie swallowed. "Okay."

"I know you don't care." He looked at her from under his lashes.

"Of course I don't care." She pressed a finger into the spot between her clavicles. He was a promiscuous being. Sometimes, Billie envisioned the legion of desirable women in her ex-husband's life. "You don't need my permission to marry, either."

"No. Of course I don't. Again, I just thought you should know."

She nodded and tried to smile more genuinely. How foolish of her to let him rattle her so. How foolish of her to put on lipstick. "Now you have told me."

"I have." He lifted his drink to cheer.

She tried not to think as she clinked her lemon seltzer to his Skipper cocktail. When Hannah caught her eyes and questioningly held up the menus, Billie shook her head once. Hannah disappeared back into the kitchen.

"Is that it?" Billie asked and set her glass down again. "If it is, I should go."

Ian held the little paper umbrella aside and drank. Wiping his mouth, he said, "Come on, Billie. Don't run away."

"I'm not running away. You told me what you came to say, didn't you? Or is there more?" She didn't want to meet his eyes anymore.

"I thought we could talk more. About us. About our lives. Now that we'll be neighbors."

"I don't... Fine." Billie sighed. If she wanted to move through her wall, maybe this was the painful way forward. "Who are you marrying?"

"Francesca," he said. "You remember her."

The name jolted her like an old thunderbolt, and she blinked as old images swam to the surface. "I remember."

"She's the one." There was pity for Billie in his smile. "We have been together on and off since you and I divorced."

Billie raised an eyebrow. "You've been together since *before* we divorced," she said. "Surely you remember that too."

"Oh, come on. Not that again. Don't be bitter. Obviously the two of us didn't work out together."

"No, we didn't." Billie didn't like how easily he brushed her hurt away. Even if it was decades old.

"So you have been sort of with her all this time." Morbid curiosity drove Billie forward. "I had you down for more of a womanizer than that."

"I'm not a womanizer. You and I—we simply didn't vibe."

"It vibed enough to make two sons."

He stood, carefully placing his napkin on the table. "I don't need to sit here, letting you call me names. You might have grown up in Mendocino Cove, Billie, and maybe you are a big deal in town. But clearly, you never left your comfort zone for a single day."

"What is that supposed to mean? Are you saying I'm limited?"

He narrowed his eyes. "In the end, *I* am the one who got an award. For, you know—doing anything at all. Not you. Me." He looked down his nose as if she was a disobedient schoolgirl, turned on his heel, and left.

Billie sat frozen to her spot. What had just happened?

"Your ex didn't leave any cash for his share of the bill, did he?" Hannah put a hand on Billie's shoulder.

The sound escaping Billie's throat was between outrage and tears.

"Never mind. There wasn't a drop in his cocktail we'd miss in this establishment." Hannah picked up his glass. "Yours is on the house, darling."

"No. No. I can..." Billie fumbled for her wallet in her purse, but her fingers knotted up.

"Don't worry about it."

"No! No. I want to pay." Billie dropped her wallet, propped her elbows on the table, and covered her face with her hands. "Sorry," she whispered. "I need a moment."

"Oh dear." Hannah sat down beside Billie and started to rub her back. "Hey...Michael? Michael! Come out here. We have an emergency."

Billie heard the restaurant's owner come over and slide out the other chair beside her. "He's a prat," Michael's deep voice said soothingly. "His movie was the dumbest, most pretentious thing I've seen in my life."

"Don't." Billie wiped her eyes with the back of her hand and shook her head. "Don't put him down to make me feel better. He's right."

"Whatever he said... I doubt it," Michael said. "Making you sit here in tears? That's not right, Billie."

Billie stood. "He's got a long-term relationship and a thriving career. He won an acclaimed award, and his face is plastered all over town. What have I done?"

"You keep this town together. We love you, Billie." Hannah sounded helpless. "Everyone in Mendocino Cove loves you."

Billie shook her head. "But what have I ever *done*?" she whispered.

It wasn't enough to have hopes and dreams. She needed to *do* something about them.

The tears started to drip again, so she blindly pulled out a few dollar bills, stuffed her wallet back in her purse, and stumbled down the stairs and out of the Mermaid Galley.

Now that Ian and Francesca would live here, she would constantly run into them.

For the first time in her life, Billie wished she could live somewhere other than Mendocino Cove.

CHAPTER 4

Of course I have time for you. No reason to thank me, Billie." Jenny shook her hair back and pulled it into a ponytail. The ferry running between Mendocino Cove and Mendocino Island wasn't fast, but the ocean breeze picked up once the white boat left the protective embrace of the cove's cliffs. "I have to teach tomorrow, but I already prepared my lecture."

Billie nodded gratefully. "Thanks, Jenny. Faye is nauseated, and Ava is waiting for a delivery of stone pavers."

"I'm glad I get to go," Jenny said cheerfully. "I haven't been to the island since I came back. But I always meant to go."

"I know." Billie turned back to watch the ferry's bow cut through the sparkling waves.

Unlike herself, Jenny *was* busy. Besides her teaching job in the history department of Elizabeth May University, she had also started her research into the lives of her ancestors. Will and Phoebe Langley had been the descendants of two large whaling families in Nantucket. They left their mark by eloping together—like proper teenagers, stealing and crashing a valuable whaling ship in the process.

After cruising the Pacific Ocean for longer than they should have, the two eventually made their home in Mendocino Cove. Determined not to have one of her descendants lose her family or comfort the way she'd endured, Phoebe started amassing a small treasure of precious heirloom items.

Billie turned back to her friend. She hadn't heard about the treasure for a while. "What happened to your heirloom items?"

"Christy took them to San Francisco to have them appraised by specialists." Jenny smiled serenely.

Agatha had hooked Jenny up with her friend, Christy, who used to work for a big auction house and still had connections in the world of arts and antiquities.

Billie wiped a curl out of her eyes. "And? What did she say?"

"She's waiting for the right people to return home from an international event." Jenny sighed. "I do hope when all is said and done, it'll be enough to buy a small house in the cove."

"Why would you do that? Isn't the hotel good enough?" Billie winked, knowing perfectly well Jenny loved her beautiful beachfront mansion.

"I still don't know whether Aunt Georgie is truly going to sell the hotel out from under us."

Billie shook her head. "That would be such a shame. I hope Georgie thinks better of selling a historic house that means so much to your family."

"She said she would. But I dearly hope her decision is not yet set in stone." Jenny's brow knitted at the thought of losing her home. "Audrey is preparing all the speeches to convince Aunt Georgie to reopen the hotel again instead of selling it. Audrey might even have a slide presentation or two."

Jenny's daughter, Audrey, had come to Mendocino Cove after graduating from one of the best hotel management schools in the country. It had been love at first sight for her and the hotel. Now, Audrey wanted nothing more than to put her talents to work and throw the doors wide open for guests.

"Did you ask Georgie for more information?" Billie wanted to know. "You should put her on the spot. After all, you'll need a bit of a heads-up in case she does want to sell since you will have to find a new place. Affordable real estate in the cove is not easy to get. Maybe more will come on the market—but I would have heard if anyone wanted to move. Right now, Ava and Christy snapped up the only two good places out there."

Ava's house hadn't even been on the market; Billie had helped her track down the billionaire owner, who lived far away and had all but forgotten he owned the property. Christy had bought the beach cottage nestled into the dunes between Billie's and Agatha's properties.

Jenny shook her head. "As per usual, I can't get a hold of Aunt Georgie. She's gone incommunicado, a skill she's developed into a fine art. At least she promised to visit the cove."

"And? Do you think she is actually coming?"

"I really don't know. She always says she'll come just to bug out at the last moment." Jenny took a stick of sunscreen out of her purse, pulled off the cap, and rubbed it over her nose and cheeks. Even though the ferry bound for the island was plowing through waves that looked like molten fire and gold, the rays of the sinking sun were still strong. She popped the cap back on and pushed the stick back into her bag. "I thought this time she sounded different, though. The passing of her last husband shook her deeply. I think she must have loved him very much."

"Fred, wasn't it? You still have white streaks on your face." Billie pointed.

Jenny wiped the excess sunscreen away, checking her hands until they were clean. "Yes, Fred. I wish I had met him. He told Aunt Georgie to come back here. I agree with him. I think she needs to come back home so she can finally heal."

"Heal from your mom's loss?"

Jenny nodded. "Georgie never got over it. I think, in sending her to Nantucket instead of keeping her at home, my grandmother might have done more harm than good."

"Who can tell," Billie murmured absent-mindedly. "My mother also told me that Georgie had to get out. Maybe the change of coast and scenery saved her sanity, such as it is. Even if her heart didn't make it all in one piece."

"It's true." Jenny sighed. "Grandma Rosie *was* scared for her. But it also allowed Georgie to bury her guilt and dark thoughts inside, something she wouldn't have been able to do had she stayed here."

"She still feels guilty?"

Jenny shrugged. "As best I can tell, you know. She doesn't exactly talk about what happened back then, and I pretty much know only what my grandmother told me. But I'm fairly certain Aunt Georgie believes it was her fault that Mom lost the trail."

"But your mom—Willow—she was the older sister, wasn't she? My impression was always that she knew the forest just as well as Georgie."

Jenny nodded. "If anything, she knew the forest better than Aunt Georgie. But that day, they were supposed to walk together, and Aunt Georgie left Mom alone. Mind you, I can't be a hundred percent sure that's how Aunt Georgie sees it. She wouldn't share her thoughts with me when we lived together in Nantucket, and certainly not after I moved to Maine." She sighed. "It could be so easy... But unfortunately, one doesn't just pick up the phone and ask my aunt Georgie things."

Billie wrapped her arms around herself. "I wouldn't want to carry that guilt."

"No." Jenny pressed her lips together and let her gaze return to the fiery ocean.

Billie let the silence—and her friend—be. The tragedy of the past was not a light topic for anyone in their small community. Even so many years later, there were still many difficult questions without answers.

Almost thirty years ago, the two Summers sisters, Willow and Georgie, had driven to one of the area's beautiful trail heads to take a walk in the majestic redwood forest.

Bobby, Georgie's spunky little terrier, had torn his collar and run off in pursuit of a squirrel or chipmunk. Upset at the thought of losing her beloved dog, Georgie left her sister to catch Bobby and return him to the car. Willow, either by agreement or because she was tired of waiting for Georgie and Bobby, walked on by herself.

At a crucial parting in the path, Willow accidentally took the wrong on. She lost the trail and strayed farther and farther into the wilderness. The official search for her was unsuccessful and eventually had to be called off. Theories about what had happened to Willow abounded until, in the end, a volunteer firefighter found her remains hidden in the shelter of a fallen tree root where she had curled up.

The small-town community of Mendocino Cove had rallied around the unfortunate family. But there was nothing they could do to help; there was no way of making it better.

The ferry's bell rang, startling Billie out of her thoughts. She straightened and hitched her purse strap higher on the shoulder. "There we are." She smiled at Jenny. "Are you okay? I didn't mean to bring up the past."

Jenny blinked, but then she smiled back and stood, holding on to the railing because the ferry was positioning itself for landing. "It has a way of popping up, doesn't it? Don't worry; I'm okay. Actually, I'm so looking forward to our little outing. I've never been to a lantern tour."

CHAPTER 5

I 've never been to a lantern tour, either. In fact, I have no idea what it is—it just sounded nice." Billie pulled out her phone and tapped on the tickets she'd bought online, suppressing thoughts of her ex, for whom she'd originally—and stupidly—bought the tickets. "There's a link to the description," she said and opened it.

"Read it to me," Jenny said.

"Okay." Billie cleared her throat. "Experience a guided evening tour inside the lighthouse tower, where lanterns are lit to showcase its historical charm." She squinted at the small words in the falling dark. "Whoops!" She wobbled as the ferry bumped against the dock, catching her phone at the last minute before it slipped from her grip.

"Hold on!" Jenny laughed. "We're almost there."

Below them, Billie spotted a young woman in a pretty boating uniform jump the small gap onto the land. Quickly and skillfully, she began wrapping the ropes around the docking bollards. When she was done, she glanced up and met Billie's eye. Billie smiled and waved, and the young woman smiled back before jostling the gangway into place and helping the first passenger safely exit the ferry.

"We'd better get downstairs too." Jenny squinted at the horizon, where the sky had turned from flaming red to lavender rose streaked with lines of burnished gold as the sun sank nearer the sea. "I'm not going to miss out on any lanterns."

"Me neither," Billie said and followed Jenny past the rows of empty deck benches, down the narrow metal staircase, over the clattering gangway, and onto beautiful Mendocino Island, home of blooming roses and quaint seaside cottages.

Once they were back on firm ground, Billie pointed. "Let's walk along the water. The lighthouse isn't too far."

"Okay. I think I remember how to get there. Sort of. It's been a hot minute."

"Same—and no wonder. It stood empty for so long. I had no idea they were working on making it accessible to the public," Billie admitted. The Donovans were usually the first to know when something interesting was happening. To be fair, most of the family lived in the cove, not the island. But the lighthouse was kind of important. It was strange that neither Billie nor Jon nor their cousins, Lex and Brock, should have heard the exciting news. It was a big deal for the small, sleepy island.

"This way?" Jenny pointed up a sandy lane veering inland.

"Yep." Billie threw a last look at the small harbor where fishing vessels in bright colors and well-used motorboats bobbed peacefully on the water.

Not so long ago, the four friends had visited the island's famous Lover's Lane. Lover's Lane was a street full of wedding boutiques, and they'd been in search of a dress for Ava's recommitment ceremony. But though they all remembered the old lighthouse at the tip of the bluff, they had only talked about what a pity it was to see the famous landmark sit empty and neglected.

"I've only been to the island a handful of times in my life," Jenny said as they climbed the bluff. "And I've certainly never been inside the lighthouse. I'm surprised we can tour it."

"Me too. It must have just opened to the public." Billie left the sandy lane and led the way toward a few large, flat stone steps leading to a field. In the softening light, she could just make out the narrow, old path that wound its way through a wild meadow.

Perched atop the rugged bluff overlooking the island's breathtaking coastline stood the once majestic lighthouse. Its proud stance told tales of endurance and resilience against storms and the elements. But time, that grand master of all, had more bite than the worst storm. It was clear that the faded old landmark was in desperate need of a do-over.

Billie stopped short, squinting up at it. "Goodness. It has seen better days, hasn't it?"

Jenny came to a stop beside her. "Sure has. And yet, there's a certain romance to it. I don't know." She tilted her head. "You know what? I like it."

"Hmm. I like it too. But I also don't want it to fall apart. It's a historic landmark after all. In the olden days, seafaring traffic depended on it for safe passage through the cliffs."

Jenny pointed. "We'd better hurry. There's already a group of people by the door."

They went on, making their way through the nodding heads of seaside daisies, wild yarrow, and beach lupines. The sea below the bluff hummed her eternal song, complemented by grasshoppers and cicadas, katydids and crickets that serenaded the warm summer night with the melodies of their kind.

The closer they got, the more details Billie could see.

The aged brick walls, kissed by salty winds and bathed in the warm hues of sunset, exuded a rustic charm she loved. Faded white paint clung to the surface, reminiscent of a bygone era when it stood proud, offering hope and guidance to passing ships.

Tall, weather-blind windows, their panes slightly warped and creaking in the breeze, revealed glimpses of a nostalgic interior. A short staircase, once polished and gleaming, now showcased faded steps leading to the landing.

Around the lighthouse grew wild remnants of a garden, and vibrant wildflowers pushed through the cracks in the stone pathway.

"It's so pretty." Jenny stopped to admire clusters of tufted sea thrift dancing in shades of white and pink. Beside them, coastal paintbrush created a stunning tapestry of fiery reds and purples.

"It really is beautiful." Billie reached out and let her fingers glide through the overgrown grasses that reached above her knee, feeling their long, wispy blades. The wind rustled through them, whispering secrets of forgotten journeys and distant adventures, capturing her imagination. The top of the lighthouse would be magical. There could not be a better spot to dream about ancient mysteries and tales whispered by the winds of the Pacific.

"Come on, Billie. Almost there."

They soon reached the group of tourists waiting for entry at the heavy door. Jenny leaned her head into her neck to squint at the top. "I wonder if it operates?"

A deep voice spoke up behind them, calm and confident. "Not since 1976. That was the last year the beacon was lit."

Billie turned around. A stranger, her age or a couple of years older than herself, had overheard them. He had his arms crossed over the chest, his silvering hair tousled from the breeze, his cobalt-blue eyes carefully hooded.

"Are you sure?" She had to tilt back her head to meet his eyes since he was a good head taller than her. "I'd swear it was 1973."

The man shrugged as if he didn't care about her opinion. "Would you mind stepping aside?"

Billie wasn't used to being so casually ignored. She frowned. Who was this stranger? She had never seen him before. Certainly, he had arrived after her and Jenny. "So you can move to the front of the line? Yes, I mind and no, I won't step aside."

"Which year was it, then?" asked one of the tourists, confused.

"1976," the man said firmly. He glanced at Jenny, hooded eyes sharp and blue as the sea, and smiled.

Jenny smiled back.

Billie frowned.

The stranger had no business giving Jenny blue glances like that. "No, no." She dug out of her purse the brochure she'd picked up on the island last time and opened it to the description of the lighthouse. "It was in 1973." She handed the brochure to the tourist, pointing to the date and glaring at the tall man who stood much too close to Jenny.

"Billie," Jenny said soothingly. "It doesn't matter."

"Oh yes, it does. This lighthouse is an important landmark on the island." Billie crossed her arms. She realized she was being a know-it-all, and she didn't really care about the correct year, but the silver fox tourist had no business standing too close and correcting her. "We locals like to get it right."

"Maybe. But the date in the brochure is wrong," the man said with a poker face. "The last beacon was lit in 1976. Excuse me. I have a tour to give." He looked at Jenny. "Hey. How are you?"

"Hey." Jenny smiled, looking nonplussed. "I'm good. Waiting for the tour to start."

The man nodded without taking his gaze off her, and now, Jenny frowned a question back. "Have we met before?" she asked, drawing out the words as if she was searching her brain for a memory.

His chest rose and sank as if he wanted to say something, but then he only shook his head. "The tour will start in a moment." Now his gaze returned to Billie. "As soon as I can get inside."

"I'm not actually in your way," Billie pointed out. There was plenty of space for him to get around her.

Without a word, the man stepped off the narrow path and into the wildflowers, rounding Billie. He stopped at the heavy wooden door, pulled an ancient-looking bearded key from his jacket, and unlocked the lighthouse. Then he stepped into the dimly lit entrance.

With a bang, the door fell shut behind him.

CHAPTER 6

"Is he the lighthouse keeper?" The tourist handed the brochure back to Billie with an offended look. "If the dates are wrong, you probably shouldn't hand this out." He turned and rejoined his friends.

"What the heck?" Billie crumpled up the leaflet and looked at Jenny. "This lighthouse *has* no keeper. The last one left ages ago. It has stood empty ever since. Just look at the peeling paint and the...the—obviously, nobody has lived here in *decades*."

"What's the old keeper's story?" Jenny put her head into her neck and looked at the top, where the lantern chamber was just visible from their angle.

"I don't really know," Billie said. "Only that his family owned the lighthouse and used to live here. I remember seeing the beacon from my bedroom. It always made me feel so safe when I fell asleep. But then it was suddenly gone. I had too much going on to really take notice. But later, I wondered what happened. My mom told me that one evening, the beacon was lit, and the next, it wasn't. It stayed dark after that and never lit again."

"Didn't they need it for the ships?"

Billie shook her head. "Even back when we were kids, it was more nostalgic than functional. The island was already using radio beacons and lighted buoys to communicate with boats and ships."

"I wonder why the light stopped so suddenly." Jenny hugged herself.

"I don't know. I can't remember hearing anything more. We didn't go to the island so often back then. The ferry only went twice a day, and there was plenty to do in the cove."

Jenny moistened her lips. "If the lighthouse is still privately owned, I guess the guy just now must be the heir. Maybe he's the son of the old keeper you remember."

Billie dropped her arms. "Don't say that. Let's hope he's just a businessman from San Fran, throwing too much money at fulfilling a fancy."

Jenny tilted her head, amused. "Why would you think that? Did you see how he was dressed?"

"Jeans and a T-shirt?"

"Exactly. Businessmen wear dark suits and crisp button-ups, not salt-sprayed jeans and sun-faded T-shirts."

"No, come on now. That's a prejudice."

"Oh, am I the one who's prejudiced tonight?" Jenny chuckled.

"They don't *always* wear suits. They—" Billie's explanation of men's business wear was interrupted by the opening of the heavy front door.

The man stepped out again, no longer wearing his old clothes. He'd put on a wide-brimmed hat that shielded his face from the sunlight and Billie's critical gaze, a comfortable-looking flannel shirt, sturdy trousers of thick cotton designed to resist wear and tear, and waterproof, rugged boots. Thrown over the marine costume was a heavy, weather-resistant wool jacket with multiple pockets.

"Good afternoon and welcome to the Mendocino Island lighthouse," he called out to the waiting group. "I'm Neil Bennett. My family acquired this lighthouse when it was decommissioned in 1874, and ownership has been passed down through generations. We have a strong connection to Mendocino Island, and we cherish its historical significance and take pride in preserving it as part of our family's and town's heritage."

"Hear, hear," Jenny said under her breath.

Billie pressed her lips together. *What?* If the lighthouse was so important to him, why had it stood empty for so many years? It didn't make sense.

Eagerly, the other visitors gathered closer around Neil. The sun had set, and in the darkening light, he truly looked like a lightkeeper from the olden times with his wide shoulders and strong chest.

"My grandfather replaced the original, non-functioning beacon light and also some other structures that were either no longer safe or needed modernization. However, mostly this lighthouse has its original parts that date back to—" Neil Bennett turned to face the other side of the small crowd and continued talking about dates and features, introducing his lighthouse while looking like he very much belonged.

Jenny was clearly fascinated by Neil, listening with intent.

Of course, Jenny was a historian, and this was her kind of jam.

But she was also dating Jon. For Billie's taste, Jenny was too smiley and too eager to question the handsome stranger. Because even Billie had to admit that he was handsome with his pepper-and-salt hair, the long, lean legs and strong arms... And those broad shoulders of a sailor were so—

Just then, Neil turned. Catching Billie's appraising gaze, he winked at her. But when he talked, he looked back at Jenny. "Would you like to see the inside now?" he asked.

Her.

Jenny.

Specifically. He'd specifically asked *Jenny* if she wanted to come inside his lighthouse.

Billie inhaled, jealous on her brother's behalf. "Yes, we would indeed," she said snippily before Jenny could answer. "Why, thanks very much. That's just what we all paid for." She pulled out her tickets and thrust them at the cheeky stranger. Neil. If that really was his name.

He looked down at her the way he had done before, as if he could barely be bothered to notice her existence. Granted, she was shorter than Jenny. Also, not blonde. Or skinny.

"Of course," he said, his face deadpan. He took Billie's tickets and ripped them, then gestured at the entrance. "Please, everyone, go ahead and gather inside the entrance room. I will guide you through the light-house in a moment."

He continued to check tickets and rip them, ignoring Billie's glare.

"Come on," Jenny whispered and pulled Billie along into the dim foyer of the lighthouse. "What's wrong with you?"

Billie's eyes widened. Jenny didn't ask people what was wrong with them. "What's wrong with *you*?" she hiss-whispered and freed her arm. "He was making googly eyes at you. What about Jon?"

Jenny let go of Billie's arm and coughed as if she were choking down laughter. "What does Jon have to do with it? I can't help it if men make googly eyes. To be fair, I don't think Neil did. Besides, dear Billie, you don't need to look after Jon and me. We'll do that ourselves."

"I don't know about that." Billie stepped aside as the man who'd handed her back the brochure bumped into her.

"Instead, take a look around," Jenny whispered. "I love the lanterns. It's so cozy. I've never been in here."

"Me neither." Billie had seen most everything on Mendocino Island, including the insides of many hous-es since she had friends sprinkled throughout the is-land's small towns. But she'd often walked past the old landmark, wondering what waited inside.

Taking her friend's advice, she craned her neck and looked around.

CHAPTER 7

Just like Neil had transformed into a lighthouse keeper by putting on historical clothes, the warm glow of softly lit lanterns cast an aura of nostalgia and authenticity that transported Billie—against her will—to another time. The last of the day's dying light shimmered through the weathered windows, mingling with the lantern light in a warm, ethereal glow and revealing specks of dust dancing in the air. Though faded and worn by the passage of time, the small entrance hall still held traces of its former maritime grandeur, and Billie's feet tingled with the desire to explore.

After the last visitor's ticket had been duly ripped, the door fell shut with a deep thud. Neil stepped into the middle of the room and started to talk about the lighthouse in a low, deep voice.

Billie tuned him out. Instead, she spent the time admiring—also against her will—the weathered wooden floor that softly creaked underfoot as if whispering tales of countless footsteps that had come before.

"Follow me, please," Neil said and looked from under hooded eyelids directly at Billie. The glance did not last long, but it let her know that he knew full well she hadn't listened to a single word of his introduction.

She blinked and looked away, feeling her cheeks warm.

She wasn't usually this rude. Usually, she was a stranger's first friend in the community. But this one rubbed her the wrong way.

"Come on, Billie. We'll fall behind." Jenny tugged on her shirt. Pulling herself together, Billie followed her.

Their group was moving deeper into the lighthouse, soon climbing a spiraling staircase adorned with ornate ironwork that led the way to the upper levels.

Billie tried not to love the staircase. But it was a losing battle. She was a sucker for anything to do with her beloved Mendocino county, and this twirling, lantern-lit center seemed like the heart of it. Each step whispered to her stories she loved: stories of full moons and silently gliding ships, raging storms and screaming crews. The handrail anchored in the massive wall was worn by the touch of hard, capable hands that sought its guidance in all the dark nights when their owners were the only ones guarding over land and people. Billie let her own smooth over the marbled wood, feeling as if she belonged.

Jenny, climbing the stairs ahead of Billie, turned to whisper over her shoulder. "It's like the air grows thick with history, isn't it? I love it. Smells delicious."

Billie wanted to say she could only smell the scent of salt water and drying driftwood but nodded instead. Because Jenny was right. Sea salt and drying driftwood were her favorite fragrances in the world. The mysterious aroma of the sea; better than flowers, better than freshly baked bread, better than anything else.

There were several levels for the group to explore. In the soft light of the romantic lanterns, the men and women listened breathlessly to Neil Bennett's stories. Maybe Billie would have liked to listen too. But now she was too far back to hear more than a particularly emphasized word here and there. She spent her time looking at the antique furnishings that dotted the rooms along the way, their upholstery faded but still exuding the naval elegance of another century.

She spotted a scruffily elegant, cozy sitting area that beckoned with plush armchairs and a cozy fireplace, ready to warm feet and hands icy from lighting the beacon at night. It looked too tempting. For a moment, Billie wanted nothing more than to sit there with a book and a cup of hot tea. Or just sit at all, just for a moment or respite from the tour and the world, just to try out. But already, the group was moving on. She threw the room a last, longing glance and followed.

At the summit of the lighthouse, Neil led them into the lantern room. Billie couldn't help but think that it truly was the crown jewel of this romantic sanctuary. Weathered brass and aged glass surrounded the visitors as they crowded in, the afterglow of the sun offering panoramic views of the breathtaking coastline and the endless expanse of the Pacific Ocean. Here and there, lantern light filtered through time-worn glass, casting gentle waves of illumination as if to prove the light-house's connection to the sea.

"It's breathtaking," Jenny suddenly whispered into Billie's ear, startling her out of her reverie. "I had no idea. I really thought it would all be cracking cement and rusty ironwork."

Billie smiled mechanically and shook her head. Not once had she thought it would be ugly up here. Somewhere deep down, she'd always known that the lantern room was this beautiful.

She stepped aside to let a large woman pass by. The soft murmuring of the group as they explored the vast, round room around the beacon light rever-berated like echoes of the past while Neil replied to questions in his soft, deep voice and told anecdotes of the dedicated keepers who once tended to the light.

Then he pointed out a glass-and-wood case of antique nautical instruments. When he moved away again, Billie went to look at it. The instruments told of adventure and exploration, and she'd have liked to touch the cool metal and turn the toothed wheels. She put a hand on the dusty glass, losing herself to her imagination and the mesmerizing sound of waves crashing against the cliffside below.

Jenny had circled the room and found her again. "Look at them," she said, putting her hand beside Billie's. "I wonder if my William and his Phoebe used instruments just like them."

"They probably did," Billie replied just as dreamily.

"Do you want a closer look?" Neil's voice suddenly asked. They yanked their hands back, but before either Jenny or Billie could answer, he pulled out a key and unlocked the glass door, opening it up and taking out a sextant. "My great-grandfather's. He used it to navigate the trade ships he captained."

Jenny took it carefully into her hands, turning it to admire the curved brass frame.

Neil pointed. "The arc is engraved with marked degrees from zero to a hundred twenty. They're the angular measurements for celestial navigation."

Billie pulled her upper lip between her teeth, her eyes going between Jenny and Neil. Did he *have* to stand so close he was practically spooning Jenny with his wide chest and big arms? And did he tell the offended brochure guy about celestial navigation too? Or was that bit reserved for the prettiest woman in the room?

"How does it work?" Unbothered by his unnecessary proximity and Billie's hostile stare, Jenny smiled up at Neil.

"There is a series of adjustable mirrors," he said and smiled back. Gently, sweetly. But he wasn't fooling Billie. She'd seen experienced con artists smile exactly like that. Neil leaned even closer, for once looking at her. "They're positioned at precise angles on the upper portion of the sextant." Again he pointed. "The mirrors reflect and capture stars, the sun, or the moon, allowing navigators to determine their position at sea."

"Aha," Billie said and crossed her hands behind her back.

Neil inhaled as if he wanted to say something but then didn't. Instead, he addressed Jenny again. "At the bottom is an arm fitted with a calibrated scale. You rotate it along the arc to measure celestial angles. And attached to the arm is a movable telescope with a small magnifying lens at one end and a crosshair at the other. It helps to find the celestial objects and align them with the horizon."

"It sounds good. But I'm afraid I still don't really understand how it works." With a small laugh, Jenny held out the sextant.

Neil took it from her hands. "Hold it steady, align the horizon with the celestial body of interest." He smiled. "In our case, the moon."

Billie glanced out the window. The moon was indeed rising, full and summer-golden. Most of the other people in their group already hung around the windows, oohing and aahing over her rise. A couple was even kissing beside one of the flickering lanterns near the entrance.

Quickly, Billie turned back to the sextant.

"Okay," said Jenny, looking gorgeous.

"By adjusting the index arm and carefully observing the position of the moon against the horizon through the telescope, we can determine the angle of elevation with great accuracy."

Jenny's smile deepened. "Okay," she said again. "Then what?"

Neil let his sextant sink. "Then you use that angle to navigate vast oceans and uncharted territories. Then, you let that angle guide you on your journeys across the seas."

"Well, I wouldn't be so sure you'll arrive," Billie said archly, turned, and walked back to the stairs.

The kissing couple scattered.

How dare he flirt so shamelessly with her friend? And Jenny? What about Jon?

"Billie? Wait."

Billie stopped and looked up. Jenny was looking down the stairs after her. "What's going on? Where are you going?"

"Out," Billie said. "I've had enough mumbo jumbo about vast oceans and uncharted territories. I'll be at the ferry port, eating ice cream."

Jenny leaned down over the handrail. "You're not mad because I'm talking with a man who isn't Jon, are you?" she whispered. "Don't worry. I'm madly in love with your brother. I just think Neil is really nice."

"You enjoy." Billie turned away, but not before glimpsing Neil, ducking back into the light room. "I'll see you at the ferry station, Jenny."

He must've heard Jenny's words.

Billie's cheeks warmed again, but she blinked her embarrassment away and turned. At least now Neil knew that Jenny was taken.

Billie climbed the last steps and let herself out into the cooling August night.

Jenny didn't follow her.

Billie was already sorry she'd stormed out like a petulant teen. But it was too late to go back now. She stopped by the edge of the bluff, looking at the moon for a moment, then turned for a last glance at the old lighthouse. For the first time in forever, the windows were lit with flickering lanterns.

Jenny still didn't come, so Billie turned and went along the narrow, sandy path to the ferry port, where she bought a double-dipped, double chocolate soft serve with extra whipped cream. By the time her gorgeous friend finally did show up, unapologetic, bright-eyed, and full of lighthouse stories, Billie had long eaten the wafer cone's last crumb.

CHAPTER 8

"The Bennett family is at least as old and established on the island as we Donovans are in the cove, my dear." Lex set down his coffee mug and raised a significant eyebrow.

Billie had invited her cousins to one of her famous breakfasts on the dock by the cottage. Brock, Lex's twin, was busy with the lumberyard that the brothers ran together, and Billie had already been afraid that she'd have to eat breakfast alone. But Lex had arrived early to help Billie set the table, and Jon was on his way to join them.

The Donovans were early risers, and the morning fog still wafted over the water that surrounded them. But the day was supposed to become beautiful, and the sun was already burning holes through the fine mist. Billie had a fleece blanket wrapped around her to ward off the Mendocino morning chill. Lex was in jeans and a T-shirt and seemed completely unaware of it.

"Are they really such an old family?" Billie had never heard about the Bennetts. And she knew a lot of people.

"Yes. Really." Lex finished a boiled egg. "Neil's grand-father was the lighthouse keeper and also captain of the ferry for...oh, at least thirty years. Neil's dad, Ray, tried to follow in his steps. He lasted ten years or so, but he was a wanderer at heart and itched to see the world. So when his grandpa died, he took Neil and left. He sold the ferry business and became a travel writer for the Mendocino Maritimes, taking shipping jobs all over the world and writing about them. What ships he captained, the ports they docked, interactions with the local people. The column was quite a success here. Can't remember now what it was called."

"Rings a bell..." The Maritimes—read *Mari-Times* in a play of words—was the local newspaper that served the island. Billie had a vague recollection of articles written by a captain, about lagoons, lobsters, and life on container ships. "I think I read his articles as a kid. I had no idea the author was from the island, though."

Lex nodded. "Ray came back home for a short while so his son, Neil, could finish high school on the island. We were in the same football team."

"But the island is not where Neil stayed," Billie point-ed out.

Lex refilled their mugs from the thermos on the table. "No. They both left again as soon as Neil graduated. Ray returned to taking on ships as far as I know, though he stopped writing."

Billie cleared her throat. "And Neil?"

Lex glanced at her. "Neil went to a maritime training academy on the East Coast. Nantucket, actually. Then he worked as a captain himself. Neil's dad passed away a couple of years ago in...Italy? Portugal. I think Ray ended up living in Portugal."

"I see." Billie sipped her steaming coffee.

Lex rubbed his chin. "Don't go picking a fight with Neil, Billie. He's good people. We were in a lot of the same sports teams while he was in school on the island, and I still think of him as a friend."

"Of course you do." Billie sighed. "Lex, he was out and out flirting with Jenny."

"That's all right," her cousin said good-humoredly. "Jenny's a terrific person. I'd flirt with her too if Jon wouldn't have such a powerful right hook."

"Stop it." Billie wanted to talk seriously. "Jon can't lose her again. He has waited all his life for Jenny to come back to Mendocino Cove."

"I doubt Jon sees it like that." Lex helped himself to another slice of bacon quiche and refilled Billie's coffee mug. "I mean, as far as sitting around and waiting for her goes. He's definitely had his share of relationships."

"We all know how those worked out for him." Billie ate the last of her chocolate croissant and rubbed the crumbs off her fingertips. "Why doesn't anybody take me seriously? I don't want my brother to lose the love of his life."

"Bills. Stop." Lex put down his quiche. "What's up with you? Ask Jon whether he's even a smidge worried about losing her. He's not. I've never seen a couple more firmly devoted to each other than those two. I expect Jon to pop the question any second. In fact,

I'm surprised Jenny doesn't already have a ring on her finger."

"She doesn't want to get married again," Billie murmured. "Her last marriage ended in disaster."

"Then she doesn't. They don't need to marry to be in love. Don't worry about it."

A deep sigh bubbled up from Billie's belly. "I'm...not," she said, surprising herself. "I'm not. Not really. I'm just...nebulously upset."

Lex helped himself to another warm slice. "Maybe it's Neil, not Jenny, who upsets you. You feel protective of the lighthouse, and you didn't know he owns it. I'm sure it feels weird to have that jumped on you without warning."

"It does feel weird," Billie admitted. "By the way, how come I didn't know about Neil? How come I don't know what's going on with one of the oldest families on the island?"

"Easy. You didn't play football when you should've."

"Be serious."

Lex shrugged. "Ray and Neil were the last of the Bennetts, and they simply weren't around for a long while. That's why."

"Maybe tell me stuff every now and then."

"Maybe ask me stuff if you want to know." Unbothered, Lex picked a chocolate croissant. "Have I told you about Gerry? He was another boy in my football team."

"I'm not interested in Gerry."

"I know. See?" He bit into the croissant.

"Does Gerry own one of the county's historical landmarks?"

"Not that I know."

"So who does?"

"Neil."

"Ugh, Lex. Really. Not Neil. Anyone else?"

"Can't remember anyone else."

Footsteps vibrated the dock, and Billie spotted Jon walking toward them. Despite the moist morning that weaved white nets around the dock and veiled the spectacular view, he was folding up the sleeves of his button-down shirt.

"Hey, Billie. Thanks for making breakfast." Jon kissed her cheek and nodded at his cousin as he pulled out a chair and sat down. "Morning, Lex."

"The man himself." Lex poured Jon a cup of coffee and grinned. "Your little sister here is worried that Neil Bennett plans on snatching your girlfriend from your tender loving embrace."

"Really?" Jon leaned back and tried the coffee. "Hmm. Well brewed, Bills. Nice and strong."

Billie glared at Lex, who grinned back even wider. "Neil was outright flirting with her in the lighthouse last night," she reported.

"Last night? What were you two doing at Neil's last night?" Jon picked a croissant and shoveled scrambled egg on his plate. "I thought she was going to do a thing with you."

"That *was* our thing. Neil was giving a lantern lighthouse tour," Billie said grumpily. "It was very romantic. There were lanterns everywhere, and Neil was explaining to Jenny how to use a sextant in the moonlight. He was practically holding her in his arms as he talked her through it."

"*Someone* should know how to use those things," Jon said and bit into his toast with honey. "It might as well be Jenny. Her ancestors were sailors, after all."

"Jon! Don't you care?"

Lex burst out laughing, and Jon grinned at Billie over his coffee mug.

"What?" She fell back into her chair.

"Neil doesn't like blondes," Lex declared. "He likes brunettes."

"What?"

"Oh, come on, Billie. Obviously, Neil was buttering up Jenny to get to you," Jon said. "He knows I'm dating Jenny. He stopped by the winery to say hi when he first came back to the island, and I showed him a photo of Jenny and me. I probably should've told you he moved back into the lighthouse. I just forgot to mention it."

"Yeah. You should've told me." Billie flushed warmly. "I didn't know who he was. I corrected him about the last year the beacon was lit. Of course I was the one who was wrong. He made me look like a fool."

"Huh." Jon shook his head but grinned.

Lex let out a hissing sound. "Burn."

"Yeah. Burn. Anyway, I can guarantee that I'm not one of the brunettes he likes. And he definitely was interested in Jenny. I could feel it."

"Well, Jenny's free to love who she wants to love." Jon helped himself to the scrambled egg and sausages. "By the way, Neil asked about you."

Billie straightened her back. "What? When he was at the winery? What did he ask about me?"

Her brother spooned copious amounts of her homemade blackberry jam on more toast. "He asked how you were," he finally said.

Billie blinked. "But why? He doesn't know me."

"Don't you remember him at all?" Lex rubbed his chin. "Maybe he was too old to register with you."

"He's older than me too. We didn't hang out much," Jon remarked. "Besides, he was an island kid. We mostly met at sporting events."

"I do not remember him. At all." Billie shook her curls.

"Anyway. Think of Neil as a friend," her brother concluded. "Don't be surprised if you see him often from now on." Jon leaned forward. "And don't worry about my love life, either. If Jenny wants to leave, she's free to do so. I won't force her to date me if she falls in love with someone else." He smiled to show that he didn't take offense.

"No, I guess you're not that kind of guy." Billie smiled back. Seeing how safe and secure her brother was in his feelings for Jenny calmed her too. "I'm sorry. I think I'm frazzled because of the whole Ian thing. He's moving back to Mendocino Cove, you know. With, uh...with Francesca."

The men both looked up. Unlike when they'd talked about Neil and Jenny, now their eyes were guarded.

Lex set down his coffee. "Francesca? The same woman who—"

"Yes, her. The same one," Billie interrupted him. She didn't need it spelled out.

Jon whistled through his teeth. "They've been together ever since?"

"That's what he said." Billie sighed.

"Are you okay crossing paths with them all the time?" Jon wanted to know.

"I guess." Under his gaze, Billie deflated. "Well, I don't exactly love the idea. But it's not like they are asking my permission to marry and move here. What can I do?"

"Nothing." Lex sighed. "Well, Faye and I sorted ourselves out after I came back. That wasn't easy either. But in the end, it worked. You'll make it happen."

"Sure." Billie nodded, but she wasn't so sure. Unlike her and Ian, Lex and Faye had been engaged, not married with kids. There'd been less. Less history, less anger, less resentment.

Lex glanced at her. "Hey, come to talk about the lighthouse and all... Neil texted me last night that he has a fundraiser event happening tomorrow. Drumming up money for a new beacon light."

Billie looked up. "And?"

Her cousin smiled. "And Jon and I are going. Maybe you should come?"

"Why?"

"Because you like the lighthouse. And because Neil is a good man. You should get to know him. I think you two got off on the wrong foot."

"Excellent idea," Jon said.

Billie sighed. She trusted Lex and Jon. If they thought of Neil as a friend... She should give it another try. After all, Donovans always stood together. "Okay," she said reluctantly. "I'll come. What sort of fundraiser is it?"

"It's called the Beacon Ball. A dance at the base of the lighthouse. The Merry Mariners are playing."

Billie liked the Merry Mariners. But... "A dance? I have two left feet, Lex. You can't be serious."

"Of course I'm serious," Lex declared. "And Billie, I won't let anyone say the Donovans of Mendocino Cove don't support the island's lighthouse keeper. You really should help represent the family. In fact, you know what? You should dance with Neil."

"I should, should I?" Billie narrowed her eyes.

"Yes," Lex and Jon said in unison. "Excellent idea," Jon added and grinned. "Now that I'm thinking about it—you kind of *have* to do it, Bills. It's exactly the show of support the island needs from the cove. But Lex and Brock and I can't very well dance with Neil ourselves."

"No," Billie said slowly. "You can only stand around and swing your long arms ever so slightly."

"That's right." Jon nodded. "And it's clearly not enough to stand around and swing one's arms at a fundraiser."

Billie looked from one to the other. Was it only her, or had things just gone Victorian? A ball and a duty to dance? What age did they live in again?

Usually it was a blessing to belong to one of the oldest families in the cove.

But sometimes, it was not.

Lex leaned forward. "Go on. Do us proud. Take one for the cove team, Billie."

"Fine," she muttered. "I'll come to the stupid Beacon Ball."

Jon also leaned forward, the grin still twinkling in his eyes. "Are you going to dance with Neil?"

Billie sighed. "If he asks, I'll dance with Neil."

CHAPTER 9

Jenny startled awake. She blinked the sleep from her eyes. The morning sun was just rising over the forgotten cove outside the window, and the first rays already danced over the wide floorboards of her room.

The phone rang again. Jenny rolled over in her big old four-poster bed and pulled it from the night-stand. "Hello?"

"Daaarling!" a tinny voice came from the speaker.

Jenny's eyes flew open. "Aunt *Georgie*?"

"I'm in San Jose, darling. In fact, I have been here for a while."

Jenny scrambled into a sitting position. "At the airport?"

"At the car dealer. I'm trying to buy a car, but it takes longer than I thought it would."

"You just walked into a dealership and said you want a car?" Jenny asked weakly.

"You should think it's easier than it is. Anyway, once I have it, I'll drive over the mountain."

"So—today? Is that going to happen today?" Jenny put a hand to her forehead. After trying for years to coax her flighty aunt into visiting, she could hardly believe her ears. "You are coming to the hotel? Today?"

"Yes. Yes, today. I told you I was going to come. Fred said I should." Aunt Georgie sighed, a sound that was both dramatic and heartfelt. "Didn't I tell you?"

"Yes, you did. But then you never arrived, and I couldn't reach you. I expected you much sooner because you said you would come after your cruise."

Their last call had been weeks ago. Jenny hadn't been able to reach her aunt for weeks and had given up hope. Too often, Aunt Georgie didn't keep her promises.

The door to Jenny's bedroom opened, and her daughter, Audrey, appeared with a wide smile on her lips. Dressed in a crisp blue shirt dress, her short hair neatly brushed behind her ears, she was clearly ready to tackle the bright new day.

In her hands was a tray with a slim crystal vase holding sprigs of blooming jasmine, a steaming cup of cappuccino, a glass of orange juice so freshly squeezed it still had foam, and an individual-sized, golden-crisp plum cake smelling like it came fresh from the oven.

Eager to share her news, Jenny waved Audrey inside.

There were definite perks to having a graduate of one of the country's best hotel management schools for a daughter.

Audrey set the tray on the large bed and sat beside it, pulling her legs up and breaking off a piece of the cake for herself.

"*Aunt Georgie,*" Jenny mouthed. Audrey's eyes widened, and she set the cake back down.

Ever since Aunt Georgie announced she was going to sell the old hotel, Audrey, who desperately needed a job to stay in the cove, had plotted ways to persuade her fabled great-aunt to reopen instead.

"I did say I was coming right after the cruise, darling, but it was a long cruise," Aunt Georgie said vaguely. "Very long. I did a lot of thinking."

Jenny had a feeling that her aunt had needed a second ocean crossing before she made up her mind to follow through with her resolve to finally return to Mendocino Cove.

"I'm glad you decided to come." Jenny nodded at Audrey. "I'll see you in a few hours at the hotel."

"Uh...at the hotel." Her aunt sounded distracted. "Aha. There's the car. See you in four hours, Jenny." Georgie hung up.

Jenny let the phone drop on the bed. "She's coming. She's really coming this time. She'll be here in a few hours."

Audrey's eyes widened, and she sucked in a breath. "I've got to get the hotel ready." She stood and picked up the tray, then set it back down. "I have to vacuum the living room and put flowers in the vases. Oh, there are dishes in the sink from baking the cakes! I should also cook something for Aunt Georgie; she'll be hungry when she gets here... What does she like to eat?"

Jenny blinked back, fighting her own sudden flutters. "I haven't got a clue what she eats, sweetheart. She used to like these German potato dumplings my grandma made... I don't know the recipe."

"I found a stash of cookbooks in the kitchen. Maybe I can find the recipe in them."

Jenny counted to three and took a large, cleansing, calming breath. "No. Don't worry about cooking, Audrey. Who knows what Georgie likes now? Maybe she's gone Paleo, or vegan, or who knows what. I have no doubt that she will tell us everything we need to know when she gets here."

Audrey nodded and picked up the tray again. "Take your coffee, Mom. Maybe get ready?"

"Sure." Jenny picked up her coffee mug as well as the plate with her cake and set them on her nightstand.

Audrey and Aunt Georgie simply had to get along. Ideally, they would like each other. And for that to happen, neither one could be scared of their relative. The Summers' were such a small family—every member was sorely needed. Now, the most important thing Jenny could do was relax both her daughter and aunt. As best she could, anyway.

She smiled. "Forget the kitchen; I'm sure it's fine if there's a baking form or two soaking in the sink." Audrey always kept it in sparkling condition.

"Wouldn't it be nice if I made cake or something?"

"Like I said, she might not eat carbs. And if she does, there is plenty of cake already, even if it is a day old. Let's enjoy ourselves instead of working and getting all frazzled before she arrives."

"Um. All right, you're the boss."

That made Jenny chuckle. Her daughter couldn't seem to help herself—from the day she'd set foot in the old hotel, she'd worked tirelessly to set up routines for everything from airing the rooms to putting fresh flowers in the vases.

Audrey claimed the work gave her joy and would make a reopening a cinch, and Jenny knew better than to complain about never having to do the dishes or cook or even make her own bed. If her daughter found joy in the tasks, she was welcome to them.

Now, Jenny went to Audrey and carefully hugged her from the side, mindful of the tray. "I'll be down in five minutes, and then we'll take a long walk on the beach. Say good morning to Polly. Okay?"

"Um. Yes. I have to…" Audrey blinked, looking like she hadn't heard a word her mother said.

"You're running lists in your head of things to prepare," Jenny remarked. "If you do that, I'm going to go back to bed. And when my aunt arrives, I'll let you manage her."

Audrey wiggled out of the hug, making the vase on her tray wobble precariously. "Got it. Okay, Mom, a walk sounds great. I should probably change; I don't look much like a graduate from a good school, do I?" Audrey turned and hurried outside, sprigs of jasmine trembling.

"It will definitely be fine," Jenny murmured. "Everything's fine. Fine, fine, fine."

She tossed back the duvet and swung her legs to the ground.

Audrey had done good, making the hotel look its best.

With everything bright and airy and beautiful, surely her aunt would not want to sell the hotel.

Suddenly the world tilted and spun in front of Jenny's eyes. "Whoa," she whispered and fell back on the bed, pushing two fingers against her temple as if it could steady the objects in the room. Slowly, like water that ebbs away, the wave of vertigo passed again.

Carefully, Jenny stood a second time, holding on to one of the bed posts. Then she went to the open window and fixed her eyes on the beach outside, concentrating on the cliff, the sea, the sand.

Her breathing slowed, and the cold sweat that had started to bead on her forehead dried in the breeze blowing in.

Her phone rang again.

"Nononooo," she whispered. Georgie could not cancel; not now, when she was already in San Jose.

With a beating heart, Jenny sat back on the bed and grabbed the phone. "Yes?"

"Mom? It's me. It's River."

"River! Baby!" Again, Jenny's hand went to her forehead. Her son was doing his medical residency on the East Coast, rarely called, and never called in the morning. "What's up, darling?" The words tumbled from her mouth. "Are you okay?"

"Yes, I'm—" He swallowed, the sound audible across the leagues that separated them. "I..."

"What?" Jenny blinked. "What happened?"

"I asked her to marry me." His voice trembled. Jenny had never heard him like that.

"You asked her to marry you," Jenny repeated stupidly. Her son had been saving for months to afford the diamond ring he'd custom-ordered for his beloved. "And?"

"And she said... She said no." He sounded like he was down in a well, the words hollow and full of echo. "She said no. She packed her suitcase and left. She's gone."

"She's gone?" Jenny couldn't quite process it. He had finally asked, and his longtime girlfriend had said no? Why?

"I don't even know where she went," River muttered.

"Are you okay?" It was a knee-jerk reaction to ask again; of course he wasn't okay.

"I was going to take off a week," River said. "I saved up all my vacation and leave days to go to the mountains with her. The mountains are off the table, but I still want to get away. I would like to come see you and Audrey. You are in Northern California, aren't you? In that old hotel? What's the town called again?"

"Mendocino Cove."

"Yes. I remember now. Will you still be there for a while?"

Jenny inhaled. "Yes, we're still here. Of course I would love nothing more than to see you, River." It'd been almost a year since she'd held her son. "And so would your sister. Please come."

"I will. Uh—I'll get back to you with the dates. I still have to see one patient through before I go. Are you sure it's convenient? Otherwise, I can try—"

"It's convenient," Jenny interrupted him. If River tried to postpone or reschedule, there was no doubt that something would come up. Another patient who needed him, a shortage of staff at the hospital where he worked, something.

"Okay." He sounded relieved. "I could really use a change of scenery, Mom."

"The beach is waiting for you. The water is cold, but we'll swim anyway. We'll walk across the bluff into town to eat clam chowder and go to the winery in the evenings to watch the sunsets. It's beautiful here. You'll see."

"She has someone else," River said suddenly, drowning his mother's last words.

"What?" The confusion in Jenny's stomach curdled into outrage. "Are you *sure*?"

"I know." He sounded sad, not angry. "She's fallen in love with someone else. A client who works with her PR company."

"Hmm." Jenny bit her bottom lip to stay quiet. She didn't know the full story. And berating River's girlfriend—his *ex*—wouldn't change anything for the better. She held the phone away so her son couldn't hear and took a couple of big, cleansing breaths.

"Maybe it was for the best," River said glumly. "Maybe there was a reason why it took me so long to ask."

"I thought at least *you* were in love with *her*," Jenny said, even more confused. "You were convinced marriage was the right path."

"I was convinced. In all honesty, Mom, it took me so long to ask because I was scared that she would say no. That in itself should've told me what I needed to know."

"Were there warning flags?" Jenny asked softly. "Something that made you feel unsure?"

"There were flags," her son replied slowly. "There were flags, and I ignored them. Listen, Mom, I'm not ready to talk about it. I'm still really upset."

"I can imagine, darling. Come here, go swimming, recover from all that work. How is that going, by the way?" Jenny was glad to change the topic. She needed to sort out her thoughts before saying more.

Because if *she* was being honest... A small glimmer of something sparked inside her. Jenny had barely known the young lady River had wanted to marry. More often than not, there had been an excuse for not meeting his family. Now Jenny understand that had been a flag too.

"Work is good, Mom. I finally met my residency accreditation requirements, and I have my license." For the first time, it sounded like River was smiling. "All that is left is my board exam."

"When is that going to happen?"

"I can take that when I'm ready. It doesn't have to be right away, but ideally, I don't wait so long I'll forget everything I learned again. Of course, I'll also have to start looking at finding a position. It's time to put my skills to work and find a job! Maybe we can talk about financing my own office, too. Only if you're game, Mom. I understand if you're not. The last thing I want to do is take a bite out of your retirement fund."

Jenny closed her eyes. She and River still had to talk about her changed circumstances. "Darling, I wish I could. But we might have to look at other options for starters."

"Oh. Of course, Mom. I don't mind working in a hospital either," River said. "Running your own place is a lot of hassle for sure."

"I'm sorry I can't help much right now, darling. I certainly would if I could."

There was a short pause. "Are you okay, Mom?" River asked. "Are you taken care of? Do you need me? I'll be there tomorrow."

Jenny swallowed. He was working himself to the bone, had just lost the love of his life, and was looking at unemployment—and still, her son wondered whether she was taken care of.

"I'm perfectly fine, darling," she reassured him. "I'm more than fine. I'm happy. But we have to sit down soon and have a long talk. My situation has changed."

"How has it changed?"

"Well, things are different now. But don't worry. Like I said, I'm happier than ever. I had a new beginning in Mendocino Cove."

"Okay. You do sound good, Mom. You sound happy." He sighed. "I'm with you."

"What do you mean?" Jenny smiled.

"My old life here is almost over. One way or the other, it's a new beginning for me too. Maybe I should start my new life in Mendocino Cove, if that's where you and Audrey are."

"Oh, River. Are you joking?" Suddenly, tears rose to Jenny's eyes. Letting kids go was so hard. The possibility of her son returning to live near her filled her heart with joy, and a warm anticipation of hearing the familiar cadence of his voice and sharing in his day-to-day triumphs and challenges. It was a chance to make up for the years when he was far away, pursuing his education.

"No, Mom, I'm not." He laughed. "Unless you don't want me."

"I want nothing more, darling. But come because you want to, not because you think you need to take care of me. I have everything I need to be more than comfortable."

"So you don't want me." Again, he laughed.

Jenny smiled, happy that there was no trace of insecurity in his laugh. He knew for certain that she loved him and wanted him. Even after his girlfriend left him, his soul and self-esteem were, essentially, intact. "I always want to have you near," she said, trying not to overwhelm him with loving assurances. "Of course I want you. Come here. There's a little hospital close by. Who knows? Maybe they'll need a new doctor soon. Sometimes, the stars align."

"Beaches, vineyards, and aligning stars? Sounds like it would be too much," he teased her.

"All right." She had to laugh herself now, but tears of joy were already rising. River was going to visit Mendocino Cove and have a look around. There was a possibility that he, like his sister, would fall in love with the beauty and the people and stay.

Maybe, just maybe, after being scattered all over the country, the Summers' would be back together. Maybe Jenny would get to have her children nearby.

She swallowed, trying not to stumble over her own hopes and dreams.

River didn't even have a plane ticket yet.

As if her son could tell she wasn't able to talk for a moment, he cleared his throat. "We'll see, Mom, all right?"

Silently, Jenny nodded.

River continued, his voice calm and firm. The way, Jenny imagined, he talked to his patients. "We'll take walks over bluffs and sit on the beach like you said. We'll have one of the beach bonfires Audrey keeps texting me about."

Jenny's voice was back. "That sounds great. I can't wait until you get here, Just, River..."

"What, Mom?"

"I should tell you that your great-aunt is coming here as well. In fact, she'll arrive today."

"The one you lived with in Nantucket?"

"Yes. My aunt Georgie."

"Is there enough space?"

"Yes," Jenny said quickly. "There's plenty of space. It's just that your aunt wants to sell the hotel. We hope she'll still change her mind. But if she does go ahead, it will take her a while to find a buyer. In the unlikely case it happens quickly, Audrey and I will find another place in town. Either way, you'll stay with me."

"Is that going to be as easy as you make it sound?"

"Well..." Jenny hesitated. "I do have a lot of friends here who are ready to help. You're still going to come, aren't you? Audrey has all the plans to talk my aunt out of selling because Audrey wants to reopen the hotel."

"I'll come," River said slowly. "I'll help you talk Georgie out of it too. If it doesn't work...at least I'll be there to help you move."

"That's the spirit."

"I'll see you soon, Mom."

"Let me know when you have dates. I love you."

"I love you too. Can't wait to see Mendocino Cove and see what Audrey's been all about."

They ended the call.

Jenny stood.

The vertigo was gone.

Right now, Jenny had other things to do than let Aunt Georgie bother her sense of balance. She had her kids to take care of.

Little or grown...kids were kids. And they needed her.

CHAPTER 10

"That's her." Audrey stood, her face pale under the summer tan. "That's Georgie's car."

Jenny stood as well. She and her daughter had been sitting on the sofa in the living room. Already, it was getting dark. The azure sky of the morning had long since changed color. A short while ago, Audrey had switched on the green Tiffany lamp by the window. The sky had turned a deep purple dotted with clouds the color of the coming night.

Nervously, Jenny glanced out the windows. The town was in desperate want of rain. But not right this minute... Aunt Georgie was scared enough of returning to the cove; she didn't need a Gothic fanfare of rolling thunder and lightning to welcome her back.

"It's her. Mom. Go let her in." Audrey sat again.

"Yes. Of course." Heart beating, Jenny hurried out of the living room and into the corridor, through the foyer with its sea-glass chandelier, and to the front door. A gush of wind pressed it open the minute she unlocked it, and there, clutching a bedazzled baseball cap to her silver curls, stood her aunt.

"Jenny," she said. "Darling!"

"Aunt Georgie!" In an instant, Jenny was twenty again. She hurled herself forward and into the arms of her flighty aunt before Georgie could change her mind again and run off, or fly off, or swim off, or disappear in any of the countless ways that had carried her away before.

But this time, her aunt caught her in her arms. She wore a silky pants suit and smelled of sun lotion and expensive perfume and also a little still like the aunt who'd held Jenny when she had nightmares where her mother lay curled into a tree root in the forest.

Her aunt's arms held her surprisingly tight and surprisingly close.

"Aunt Georgie," Jenny whispered and closed her eyes. "You finally came."

"I said I would, darling," her aunt said soothingly, the way you talked to scared children, and, for a moment, enveloped Jenny in fragrant silk. "I said I would come, didn't I?"

Her arms gently loosened their hold.

Stepping back, Jenny straightened and opened her eyes again. "Yes. You did say that, Aunt Georgie."

For a moment, she'd been younger than her aunt. For a moment, her aunt had taken care of her.

Usually, it was the other way around.

After her sister, Willow, died, Georgie had been too distraught to function. A teenage Jenny had taken care of Georgie as much, if not more, than Georgie took care of her. Later, after they each chose the path that they wanted to walk in their new Nantucket life, their hold on each other had loosened. So much so that for decades, they had not seen each other and barely talked on the phone.

"Well." Aunt Georgie pushed her manicured hands into the silk suit pockets. "The old house still stands, then."

"Yes." Jenny took another step back. "It still stands. In fact, it's doing great."

"Hmm." Georgie nodded. "Well, I have a suitcase in the trunk."

"We'll get it later. First, come inside, Aunt Georgie." She held out a hand. "My daughter Audrey is waiting inside. She's scared to meet you."

Aunt Georgie tilted her head. "She's scared? Why is she scared?"

"Because you are a formidable creature. As you know very well." Jenny smiled, still holding out her hand. "Just look at you. Out of the pages of a fashion magazine. Who would not be intimidated by so much fabulousness?"

"Well. Sure." Finally, Georgie smiled back, and then she took Jenny's hand. "Let's go relieve your daughter of her intimidation then. Audrey, is it?"

"Yes, Audrey. That's right."

Jenny led her aunt into the hotel, letting go of her hand only after the heavy front door closed with a firm thud behind them.

Georgie looked up. "Pop's old chandelier," she said softly. "I forgot it existed."

"It's been here all this time, waiting for us to come back." Jenny flipped the switch, and the chandelier glowed in all the soft glory of the sea. Sweet, foamy whites, glassy greens, opaque hues of blues as mysterious as the depths of the ocean lit up the room.

Jenny watched her aunt's eyes widen with appreciation. "Come on in, Aunt Georgie. You had a long drive. Let's make you comfortable." She crossed the foyer and flipped on the light in the corridor. "Audrey is in the living room."

"Hmm." Aunt Georgie sounded as if she either doubted that's where her great-niece was, or that she herself could get comfortable. But her footsteps echoed behind Jenny's as she followed her.

Jenny's gaze met Audrey's when she entered the living room. She nodded reassuringly at her daughter. The cozy fire they'd built earlier still crackled in the grate, and Audrey had switched on more of the small lamps that dotted the tall room. She had also drawn a few of the pretty, sheer curtains in front of the long row of window doors leading onto the beach.

"Darling." Aunt Georgie stepped around Jenny and held out her hands. "You're my great-niece, aren't you?"

Audrey nodded, putting her hands into those of her great-aunt. "It's so nice to meet you, Great-aunt Georgie. How are you?" she asked politely.

"All right." Georgie flashed Audrey a quick smile. "You remind me of someone."

"I do?"

"Hmm."

Jenny looked from her aunt to her daughter and from her daughter back to her aunt.

How had she never seen it before? Had she been blind?

All this time, she had thought Audrey looked so much like Willow. But now...

Audrey pushed back a strand of her blonde bob, and Jenny blinked again.

Her daughter's hair had grown out to about the same length Georgie sported, and in the soft light muted by colored glass shades, the color looked as silver as Aunt Georgie's own.

The slope of the nose, the hollow of the cheeks, the dip in the chin... Audrey looked like a younger, sweeter Georgie.

But the long, graceful neck was that of Willow. The determined blue of the eyes, the lithe body of an Amazon...those were all Willow.

Suddenly, Georgie's smile dropped, and she let go of Audrey's hand. "I'm tired." Her eyes and voice changed. "I'm really, really tired."

"Of course you are." Jenny was startled at the sudden difference in her aunt. A moment ago, she had been pleased at rediscovering the sea-glass chandelier and meeting her great-niece. Now, she looked thirty years older.

"It's been a long drive." After all, her aunt wasn't a spring chicken anymore. Jenny had been surprised when Georgie announced she was going to drive over the mountain herself.

"It was a very long drive." Aunt Georgie seemed to collapse more into herself with every passing second. Her shoulders drooped, pulling wrinkles into her expensive suit jacket. "How about the rooms upstairs? Are they habitable?" Her voice was quiet, every word an obvious effort.

"They are." Clearly hurt by what must have seemed like sudden rejection from Georgie, Audrey frowned.

Jenny gave her daughter a reassuring nod, and then she put an arm around her aunt. "Audrey got your room ready," she said softly. "Let me show you. How about a hot bath and a nice cup of lavender tea before you go to bed?"

Georgie's back rounded as if the weight of Jenny's arm was too much. "Does the window look out on the beach?" she murmured.

"Of course it does. Come on. Let's get you settled."

Jenny had told Audrey what room to prepare for their aunt. Not one of the ones the family used to use, but the biggest guest room. There were enough memories waiting in the cove without Georgie sleeping in her old bed.

Wordlessly, her aunt followed Jenny upstairs.

Maybe Georgie could buy a car cash down and drive herself over the mountains.

Maybe she could sell the hotel on the spur of a moment if she wanted to.

But the stairs up to the bedrooms—maybe Georgie couldn't do those. Several times, she stopped. Jenny started to doubt they would ever reach the top. There were fits and starts and pauses and big inhales and sighed exhales, and none of them had anything to do with bad knees or a wobbly hip.

Meanwhile, night fell onto the mansion like a down blanket. No longer did light fall onto the stairs through the large window; the black outside was tinged the color of ripe summer plums and blackberries. Thunder growled, and when Aunt Georgie finally reached the landing, lightning streaked across the sky.

"Are you okay?" Jenny frowned at the window. Mendocino Cove was suffering from a long drought. Why did the weather have to be dramatic this night of all nights? Why not show her aunt a sweet, star-sprinkled view from her window to welcome her back and make her comfortable?

"I miss Fred," Georgie gasped between gulps of air as if the stairs had been a steep mountain.

"I know. I'm so sorry for your loss."

Georgie nodded. "Well, which one's mine?"

"This one here." Jenny took a few steps down the corridor and opened the door.

A small smile tugged on Georgie's lips. "The big one, huh?"

Jenny smiled back. "You do own this place. The least we can do is give you the nicest room."

"Where do you sleep, darling?"

"In my old room."

Georgie sighed one more time, but her legs seemed to work just fine once more when she walked into the room.

Jenny followed her. Audrey had spruced the room up; everything was fresh and clean and smelled like wildflowers on a breezy day. Already, Jenny could hear her daughter bring up the luggage she'd found in Aunt Georgie's car.

"Can I come in?" Audrey stood in the door, questions in her eyes and a suitcase in each hand.

Jenny nodded. "Thanks for bringing up the luggage, sweetheart." She stepped aside to free the way.

Georgie, who had silently studied the room, turned. "Thank you, darling."

"Of course." Audrey set down the suitcases and looked her great-aunt in the eyes.

Willow's eyes.

"Uh..." Jenny put a hand on Georgie's arm. "What about that bath?"

Georgie relaxed. She was no longer drooping, the way she'd done downstairs. "Good idea." She took a step back from Audrey—or maybe, Jenny hoped, it was not a step away from her daughter but a step deeper into the cozy room.

Audrey folded her hands in front of her. "There's a carafe of fresh water on the nightstand. Is there anything I can get you?"

"Noooo..." Georgie needed an entire sentence made of *no* as she considered the offer. "No, I'm good. Thank you. Good night, darling."

Audrey's face fell, but she quickly rallied a smile. "Good night." She turned and walked out of the room.

Jenny suppressed a sigh. "I'll leave you to it. Good night, Aunt Georgie."

Her aunt nodded. "Don't wake me tomorrow morning."

"All right. Sleep tight."

Jenny went to the door. She could hear Audrey's light steps on the marble stairs. "We'll talk tomorrow." She left no space for doubt in her words.

They would talk.

There was a moment of silence before she received a response. Then her aunt said softly, "Good night, darling."

CHAPTER 11

The morning fog that pooled over the sand of the Forgotten Cove was as pale and bright as ice. Sunrays only started to poke through in spots here and there, but the patio stones still radiated yesterday's heat.

"Should we wake her?" Audrey set her unused napkin—now folded into a swan instead of a hedgehog—on the table.

Jenny pushed the good china plate in front of her aside and propped her elbows on the table. The sea's scent of fresh seaweed, glistening pebbles, and hidden sand dollars called to her.

"Aunt Georgie's had a long day traveling yesterday," Jenny said. "Let's give her another ten minutes to show up for breakfast. Then we'll check her room to make sure she didn't run away again during the night."

"Okay." Audrey scratched a mosquito sting on her cheek. "Mom, does she not like me or something? I got the feeling last night."

Jenny picked up her mug and took a sip. Her daughter had brewed delicious coffee, but once poured, it cooled quickly.

"Don't drink that," Audrey said. Leaning forward, she took Jenny's cup and tossed the contents into the potted hydrangea. It had become a habit of hers, and the plant thanked her by growing flowers as blue as the summer sky. Audrey refilled the cup with steaming coffee from the silver thermos and handed it to Jenny.

Jenny took it and smiled her thanks. "Aunt Georgie doesn't know you yet," she said. "Therefore, she cannot like or dislike you." Leaning back, she studied her offspring. Then she covered Audrey's hand that still lay on the table with her own and squeezed. "Hang on a moment." Sipping her piping hot brew, she stood and went through the open French doors into the living room.

The heirloom armoire was mostly empty of the treasure her ancestors had collected, but the family photo albums were still there.

Jenny pulled out a yellow one, which held a small handful of pictures from her childhood. She tucked it under her arm and returned to the breakfast table.

Audrey's napkin swan had changed into a crumpled ball. "What have you got there?"

"Photos. Here, look at this." Jenny set down the cup and album, then pulled one of the wide wicker chairs close to her daughter and sat. She opened the album and pointed to an aged photo that the sun had bleached into monochrome sepia.

Jenny tilted her head, trying to see the photo through her daughter's eyes.

Two girls in old-fashioned bikinis lay on their bellies on a beach blanket, ankles crossed in the air, heads in their hands, joyously smiling for the photographer. A small, bright-eyed Jack Russel terrier was standing beside one of the girls. His paws were dusted in sand; his tongue hung in a cheerful, panting canine grin.

Audrey leaned closer. "Who is this?" She squinted, puzzled.

"That's my mom." Jenny pointed to Willow.

"You haven't shown these to me yet!" Audrey shaded the picture from the sun glaring at the vanishing fog. "Gosh. She looks like you in this picture!"

"She looks more like *you*." Jenny smiled. "I did too, especially as a teenager. I'm older now than she ever got to be. But who knows? Had she lived, maybe we would still look alike."

"Then this is your Georgie?" Audrey pointed to the other girl. "Yeah." Her smile fell a little.

"That's right," Jenny confirmed. "Who does she look like, kiddo?"

"Me," Audrey said slowly. "I look a lot more like Georgie than Willow. You look more like your mom, though."

"I agree. I didn't really notice how much you resemble Aunt Georgie until last night when the two of you stood next to each other." Jenny tapped on the foil that protected the old photo. "But it's uncanny."

Audrey fell back in her chair. "Weird. But good, too. Georgie still looks fabulous, and I'll be lucky if I look like her when I turn sixty."

"Shrimp and plenty of swimming," Georgie's voice announced loudly from the French door. "That's the secret recipe, my sweet darlings."

Startled, Jenny looked up. Her daughter's faint *oh* barely registered through her own surprise. "Aunt Georgie! Good morning." She put a hand over the photo, instinctively covering the picture of the happy, beach-bound sisters.

"You *do* look like me, child," Aunt Georgie declared. Last night's feebleness had disappeared. She was dressed in a wide, blindingly white blouse, wide, navy-blue linen pants, and straw wedges. Linen fluttering behind her, Aunt Georgie sailed toward them with all the majesty of a frigate. "And I don't mind saying that you are right. *Good* for you." She winked at Audrey.

Audrey's hands untied the napkin starfish in her hand. "Right," she said, her voice uncertain. "I suppose I got lucky."

"You sure did." Her great-aunt sounded highly satisfied.

"All right, I'm glad we're all happy with the way we look." Jenny smiled at Aunt Georgie's reaction to overhearing the conversation. "Sit down, Aunt Georgie. Do you want coffee? Audrey made an excellent—"

"Yes," Aunt Georgie interrupted and sat down. "I bet she did. Yes, I want coffee. Oh, do I."

Jenny exchanged a look with her daughter, who nodded graciously, stood, and poured.

"Thank you, child." Aunt Georgie sipped and nodded, then reached across the table and patted Jenny's hand.

"I can practically see what you're thinking. You think all my men and money have turned me rude."

"I have not thought anything of the sort. Your mind cooked that up all by itself, dear aunt," Jenny said politely. She loved her desperado-aunt too much, and she knew Georgie wasn't rude. Just...thoughtless, sometimes. Stormy. Flighty, since the death of her sister. And Aunt Georgie had always been the smart one. Rarely did she do something she wasn't aware of doing.

"I'm still the same I always was," Aunt Georgie declared as if she knew where Jenny's thoughts had wandered. "So, you two. Relax. Stop trying so hard. You don't need to impress me."

"We don't?" Jenny asked and raised an eyebrow.

They *had* hoped to impress Aunt Georgie.

"No. Jenny, darling, I love you to bits without you trying. You know that."

"I do?" Jenny smiled to soften the words.

"Yes. Uh. You do."

"Oh." Jenny didn't *exactly* know that since Aunt Georgie had been avoiding her for decades. "But good because I love you too. And hearing it makes me feel warm and happy inside."

"That's probably the coffee, darling." Aunt Georgie turned her head. "Audrey, child—you're obviously a great host, and I can tell that you would be fantastic at running a hotel. By the way, I never doubted it for a minute, so you don't have to spoil me to prove it. Unlike the rest of us, you clearly inherited my mother's knack for hospitality."

"Thank you." Audrey still looked uncertain.

"In short, I want you two to take a big, calming breath." Aunt Georgie eyed the many offerings on the table. "I'm not going to sell the hotel right this minute."

"You're not?" Jenny's hand was still covering the photo.

Aunt Georgie didn't reply but leaned toward her. "What are you hiding there?" Diamond rings sparkled on her fingers as she pushed Jenny's hand aside.

Aunt Georgie's pupils dilated, then shrank into pinpoints. "Oh." She turned away.

Hastily, Jenny closed the album and stowed it out of sight on her lap.

Aunt Georgie's mouth was a thin line. She had never forgiven herself for leaving her sister that day in the redwood forest.

Audrey had noted the change in Georgie's mood. "If we would reopen the hotel," she said quickly, "I could make themed breakfasts."

Georgie turned unseeing eyes on her great-niece. "Themed."

Audrey nodded. Jenny stood and returned the album to the armoire while her daughter explained. "Yeah, like beach-themed, or seaside-themed."

"How would that look?" Aunt Georgie's voice sounded mechanical. Clearly, her mind was far away.

"Like today, I made ocean-blueberry pancakes," Audrey pointed out. Jenny took her seat again and nodded encouragement.

"What are...what? Ocean what?"

"Um, ocean-blueberry pancakes. They're just blueberry pancakes topped with a drizzle of blueberry syrup to look like ocean waves."

"And?"

"And...I also make seashell-shaped waffles, served with whipped cream and fresh fruits." Audrey pointed to the carefully folded waffles. She'd gotten up with the birds to make them, as Jenny knew. "We could also offer...maybe a Sandy Beach Parfait, a layered parfait with granola, yogurt, and local fruits from the farmers market."

"Or Sunrise Smoothie Bowls," Jenny helped out. "We'll blend tropical fruits and top them with mango and pineapple to look like a sunrise over the Pacific Ocean. Aunt Georgie, did you know? Audrey's specialty is what she calls the Lighthouse Breakfast Burrito. She uses black bean sauce and baked cheese to make it look like a little lighthouse."

"Oh." A spark of interest lit Aunt Georgie's eyes. "Fun."

"I saw it on the internet and thought it was a cute idea," Audrey admitted. "I have a ton of other ideas as well. I have written out an entire breakfast list. We could offer guests two or three different options every day."

"What guests?" Aunt Georgie blinked.

Jenny put a hand on her aunt's ring-laden fingers. "Never mind. What do you feel like for now? Sweet breakfast, or savory?"

Suddenly, Georgie's wicker chair scraped back, and she stood. "Nothing. Thank you. I usually only have coffee to watch the...the old waistline. It...uh..." She frowned at the breakfast. The table was gorgeously set, with blue hydrangea flowers, trays and plates and stands full of delicacies, and thin china shimmering like delicate seashells.

Jenny stood too. "Aunt Georgie, my dear."

"What?" Her aunt looked up.

"My daughter made a special breakfast for you, and you can't even enjoy it."

"No," Georgie said, sounding hopeless. "I'm sorry, darling. I don't think I should be here after all. In this town. On this patio." She turned a sparkling bracelet on her arm. "I didn't sleep a wink."

Jenny went to her aunt and put an arm around her shoulder. "Mendocino Cove is our home. Didn't Fred tell you to come here?"

"He did. Maybe he was wrong."

"He loved you. Didn't he?"

Mute, Georgie nodded.

"I love you too. I think instead of running from the memories of my mother, we should tackle them."

"Tackle them? Tackle memories? It's not possible, Jenny, darling. Believe me, I tried. It's no more possible than tackling fog or the ocean. It can't be done."

"Let's try doing it together." Jenny pulled her aunt into a proper hug. "Let's see if that makes a difference."

"Do I have to talk about the past?" Georgie's muffled voice came from Jenny's shoulder. "I don't want to talk. I've had enough therapy to last me the rest of my days."

Jenny let go so she could look in her aunt's eyes. "It might be helpful to talk about the past," she admitted.

"Then I tried and failed." George's throat moved as if it remembered the words it had formed. "I really did, darling."

"Hmm." Jenny pressed her lips together to think. To move past her guilt, Georgie had to face the past. How could she do that without talking about what had happened?

Another chair scraped over the tiles of the patio. "Maybe," Audrey said softly as she stood and started to stack the unused plates, "Maybe you two could take a walk."

"A walk?" Jenny looked at her daughter. Audrey knew everything Jenny knew about the time Willow went missing. "You think we should walk along the beach?"

"No." Audrey lifted the stacked plates in one hand and a tray heaped high with her Coastal Crab Omelets in the other. "I think you two should take a walk in the forest. On the trail where it happened."

Georgie looked aghast.

"Think of Fred," Jenny said. "Think of how much he loved you, and you him, and think how much *I* love you. Should we try it? If talking didn't help, maybe walking will."

Her aunt exhaled as if she'd already climbed the steep mountain trail. "Absolutely not."

Jenny tilted her head. They had to do *something*. Otherwise, her aunt would simply run away again from her old trauma. "I think we should," she insisted gently.

Georgie sighed. "I think we should too. But I hate the trail. I hate what happened."

"But it's over. It already happened," Audrey said quietly. "It's already over. Now you have to save yourself."

For a long while, Aunt Georgie looked at Audrey.

Maybe she was seeing Jenny's daughter. Maybe she was seeing herself, the way she'd looked when she was young and happy and had her sister at her side.

Audrey didn't look away, and she didn't flinch under her formidable aunt's stare.

"I'll try it," Aunt Georgie finally said and broke eye contact. "For you two, I'll try. Worst case, I'll hate seeing the forest again."

"Best-case scenario, seeing it again will tackle the fog and the ocean," Jenny finished the sentence. "Sometimes, it starts with a single step."

Audrey held up her tray. "Would you like an omelet before you go, Great-aunt Georgie?"

Georgie eyed the succulent folded triangles. "Willow loved omelets for breakfast. Did you know that, Audrey?"

Audrey lowered the tray again. "I'm sorry."

Aunt Georgie shook her head. "I'll need energy if you are making me do exercise." She picked up an omelet with her bare fingers. "I haven't eaten one of these in ages." She took a bite, and her eyebrows rose in surprise. "Oh. It's good!"

"There we go." Jenny also took one of the luscious triangles. The trail hike was long, and she'd need energy to brace her aunt. "Come on. Let's clear the table and leave before it gets hot. We'll take my car."

CHAPTER 12

T he trailhead looked familiar. Not long ago, in a ghostly echo of the past, Jenny and her friends had been searching the majestic redwood forest up here for Faye. Unlike Willow, Faye had not lost the trail—but the hours she'd been missing had been dramatic anyway.

Now, Jenny was with Aunt Georgie as she stepped into the redwood forest. They'd both changed into long pants and shirts to protect themselves from bugs and sunburn. But while the sun had burned away the fog, the bugs were still asleep in the moss and huckleberry bushes.

"I knew the trees were tall," Aunt Georgie said, voice hushed in awe at the beauty of the wild forest. "But I didn't remember how straight they are."

"I was here only weeks ago, and I forgot too. It's as if my brain can't wrap itself around these trees." Gripping her bottle of water, Jenny tilted her head back, squinting up.

The trunks reached up to the sky, their branches intertwined into a canopy of deep-green foliage. Jenny could taste the moisture of the air as she breathed in its sweet, earthy scent. Sunbeams fell through the leaves, creating a magical atmosphere full of wonder and discovery that lured visitors deeper into the forest.

Jenny took a deep breath, eyeing the enchanting wilderness that was so perilous. "Shall we?"

Aunt Georgie started walking in the same halting way Jenny had seen before. "It's pretty, but it does give me anxiety coming back here. I never ever wanted to see this trail again."

"At first, I had trouble walking here as well," Jenny admitted. "But then something happened with a friend of mine, and I *had* to go down the trail—and now I understand that it wasn't the trail's fault. Does that make sense?"

"I don't know."

Tall, feathery ferns started to replace the lush wood sorrel, and the bubbling of a creek could be heard. The path was wide and sloped down, making for easy walking. Still, Aunt Georgie's breathing sounded as if she was out of breath, and her face was flushed. "I never thought it was the trail's fault. I always thought..." She stopped and wheezed.

Here it comes, Jenny thought and stopped as well.

"What did you think?" she asked softly.

"That it was my fault."

Jenny inhaled to reply.

Aunt Georgie held up a hand. "I know. I know what you're going to say."

"It wasn't your fault." Jenny exhaled. "It wasn't your fault, Aunt Georgie."

"A thousand therapists told me that." Aunt Georgie coughed asthmatically, then doggedly resumed walking. "For years and years, people told me that it wasn't my fault." She touched the bark of a redwood as she passed. "And yet, darling. If I had stayed with Willow, she would not have lost the trail. I could have prevented what happened, had I picked my sister over my dog. And so, in conclusion, it *is* my fault."

Jenny's heart was beating harder than their sloped path warranted. After the first few days of tumbled stories and memories she'd spilled to help the search party find her sister, Aunt Georgie had never again talked about the day Willow got lost.

Was it really that clear-cut? If Aunt Georgie hadn't left, Jenny would have had a mother?

"See?" Aunt Georgie sighed. "You know it was me too."

"No." The word came too quickly to sound believable. Jenny tried again. "Maybe it is true that nothing would have happened had you two stayed close. But was there a reason for you to expect Mom would leave the trail?"

"I want to say no so badly," her aunt murmured and slowed her pace. "But if I'm honest, I can't say no, Jenny. I can't do it because she did leave the trail. I'm not fond of science, but facts are facts. And the fact is that Willow lost the trail."

"But you didn't know she would," Jenny repeated helplessly. "Had you known, of course you wouldn't have turned around."

"I can't even say *that* much." Aunt Georgie's voice was only a whisper. "We had an argument in the car. I was driving, and I thought she held Bobby too tightly. He was squirming. I was mad, and she was annoyed because he tried to wiggle out of her arms. We argued."

The ferns had grown taller and fuller, and now they reached the creek. Like a shiny animal, it bubbled and giggled, telling stories nobody could understand anymore.

Jenny stopped at the creek bed. Had her aunt left Mom on purpose? "You had an argument? About what?"

Aunt Georgie shook her head. "I honestly can't remember; something stupid that didn't matter in comparison to what I felt when she didn't come as expected to meet me at the car. I ran along the entire trail to search for her. First, I was worried. Then I was scared, and then... I don't know if you believe me, but it took me years to even remember that we *had* an argument. That's how unimportant it had been."

"Aunt Georgie..." How could she forget something as important as an argument? Had Willow been so upset she forgot to concentrate on the trail?

"I'm being honest, Jenny. It must have been something petty and stupid, like the way she held the dog or talked to him or something like it. I racked my brain, and I couldn't put it together again. It wasn't unusual; we were sisters, and we were so different from each other. We often bickered. If it had been a big argument, I would remember it. Right?"

"I don't know." Jenny didn't trust herself to say more. What if Georgie was at fault after all? She rubbed her face with both hands to rid herself of the dawning suspicion. "Even if you *did* fight... Aunt Georgie, unless you meant to upset Mom so much that she'd get lost, it still wasn't your fault. You are allowed to fight, and you're even allowed to go after your dog."

For a while, they walked along the bubbling creek in silence.

Then Georgie said, "It means a lot, hearing that from you, my darling. Listen, I need to sit down. I'm in good shape, but I am old."

"Of course." Jenny pointed at the fallen trunk of a young tree. "Let's sit on it. The split in the trail isn't far now." It was at the fork, they thought, that Willow went the wrong way. The left turn led back up the mountain and soon, back to the parking lot. Take the right turn, and the path meandered deeper and deeper into the vast forest before eventually turning back. But this longer loop was less wide and less obvious. If Willow had thought she was on the short loop, she might easily have gotten confused, thought she lost the trail, and gone to look for a shortcut back to the car. Once turned around, the forest became a maze of trees that no longer seemed governed by the laws of north and south, east and west.

With a groan, Aunt Georgie lowered herself on the smooth bark of her seat.

Jenny found a spot beside her. She looked around and took in all the details—the lush green trees, the sunbeams that shimmered through their branches, the birds singing in harmony.

"She was so full of life back then, running ahead with her wild ideas and dreams," Aunt Georgie said suddenly.

Jenny nodded. "Mom was a free spirit."

"For sure." Georgie shifted her weight, trying to get comfortable. "I tried hard to learn who your father was, by the way. Maybe that's what we fought about. We often did. It hurt my feelings that she didn't confide in me."

"Hmm." Jenny had asked too. But the stubborn look on her mother's beautiful face had taught her quickly that she was wasting her time. "Not to be shocking and all, but maybe she didn't know who my dad was," she suggested.

Surprise pulled back Georgie's chin. "Darling! What nonsense. Of course she knew. She was madly in love with your dad, whoever it was. We were good girls back then. I mean—sort of. We were no longer teenagers when it happened, after all."

"Good girls." Jenny smiled. Despite Grandma Rosie's firm hand and prim expectations, Willow had been a true child of nature. Her soul, Grandma Rosie always claimed in a half adoring, half exasperated tone, was made of the same stuff as waves and stars and fireflies.

The corner of Georgie's lip lifted too. "Believe it or not, but until my twenties, I *was* a good girl. I tried to make Mom proud."

"Really?" It didn't seem likely. Aunt Georgie had been married several times, and even though Jenny loved her aunt, she had often secretly thought she was flighty and irresponsible.

"Really. I think I tried to compensate for the trouble my older sister caused. Well, I've given up on being good since then."

"Hmm." Jenny peered at the tips of her sneakers.

"I don't mean *you* when I say trouble, darling." A smile brightened Aunt Georgie's voice. "I mean your mother. You can bet that Rosie was upset when her eldest came home and declared she was pregnant. It wasn't the thing to do back then."

"Nobody ever talked to me about any of that," Jenny said, unable to keep the accusation from lilting the words. "Not you, not Grandma, and certainly not my mother."

"No. We wanted you to be happy, not worry about mysteries." Aunt Georgie smiled. "Of course Mom threw herself into Willow's cause. It wasn't long before she started to see her own daughter in the women who stayed with us. She and I—we never got over losing Willow." Aunt Georgie's voice faded into silence. "You were the strongest of us."

Jenny looked her aunt in the eye. "I didn't have a choice, Georgie. I had to be strong."

Aunt Georgie's throat moved as she swallowed. "I know. That's another thing for which I hoped therapy would help. I failed you. I know I did."

"We did the best we could," Jenny said after a while. "I firmly believe we all did the best we could."

Her aunt nodded. "That we did. Every morning, I tried to do better. But I could barely look into your eyes, knowing it was me who had cost you your mother. I really thought I would break into pieces. A thousand sharp shards."

Jenny knew how it felt, and now it was her who didn't like to remember. She jumped off her seat. "Let's keep going."

Aunt Georgie stood. "My joints are creaking like a pirate ship." She gave a wan smile as she shaded her eyes. "We're almost at the bend in the creek where I turned around."

Something rustled in the bushes on the other side of the creek.

Jenny turned. There were mountain lions in the forest, and not long ago, Gabe and his men had busted a hidden illegal marijuana farm.

Georgie gave a small, startled gasp. "Oh! Oh!"

"What?" Jenny wheeled around.

Georgie held out a shaking finger, pointing at the tall, dark-green fronds of a large sword fern. "Look. It's Bobby. I'm going to be sick."

"It's only a little Jack Russell terrier. Of course it's not your Bobby." Jenny took her aunt's arm, but she could feel the effect of seeing the small dog that looked so much like Bobby here, on this path, too.

"Ugh." Aunt Georgie pressed a hand to her stomach. "I don't feel good."

The ferns rustled again, but this time, Jenny could discern the form of a man. "Hey." He stepped on the path, brushing leaves and grass seeds off his shirt.

"Neil!" Jenny closed her eyes for a brief moment, savoring the relief washing through her. "You scared me."

CHAPTER 13

I didn't mean to scare you, Jenny. Hey, pup, come here. Come get a treat." Neil whistled, and the little terrier, tail wagging, came jumping toward him. Neil fished a bit of kibble from a pocket and rewarded his dog, then hooked a leash onto the collar.

"He looks like a dog I used to have," Georgie said weakly. She still looked pale. "He spooked me, running out of the bushes like that. Who are you?"

Neil turned to her. "I'm Neil. Sorry about that; I shouldn't have let him off the leash."

"Neil's the lighthouse keeper on Mendocino Island." Jenny patted Aunt Georgie's arm. "He just moved back home."

Neil looked between them. "Diggory here ran after a chipmunk, and I went after him. He usually comes when I call, but he's only a puppy. Sometimes, he forgets."

Georgie put a hand to her heart. "I'm glad you found your dog." A big breath swelled her chest. "They run fast, and the forest is big."

Jenny glanced at her aunt. The dog really did look very much like Georgie's Bobby. Only Bobby had had the first gray hairs in the muzzle when he ran away, and this dog was still young.

"Are you alone, Neil?" Jenny asked to guide the conversation in a different direction.

He nodded. "It's just me and little Dig, taking a walk. We heard you coming. I thought we were farther ahead when I left the trail—I didn't mean to jump out like this. You must've thought I was a mountain lion."

Jenny tilted her head. The stories of illegal marijuana growers jumping out of the brush to attack Faye and Gabe floated through her mind again. But she liked Neil, and he was the lighthouse keeper, one of their own. "It's all right. No worries." She smiled, glad it had turned out so well.

Neil smiled back. "Are you sure? You seem upset."

Diggory pulled on his leash, and Jenny kept pace with Neil as he allowed the dog to pull him a few steps away from the trunk where Georgie was sitting.

"It's not mountain lions we were scared of," Jenny told him. "Thirty years ago, my aunt lost her own dog on this path. She left the trail to find the dog. Her sister walked on by herself and disappeared into the forest."

Neil turned to her. "Willow Summers. The woman who lost the trail."

"Yes. Willow was my mother. Did you hear the story?"

Neil exhaled. "It was my dad who found her. Ray Bennett."

Jenny had forgotten the name of the volunteer fireman who had finally found her mother. But now she remembered. "Ray! Of course. He was your dad?"

"Yes, he was." Neil glanced over his shoulder. "What are you two doing here?"

"My aunt never forgave herself for going after her dog that day," Jenny said quietly. "In her mind, it is her fault my mother lost the trail. Of course it wasn't...but knowing doesn't always heal the heart."

"I agree." Neil nodded. "A lot of people were traumatized back then."

Jenny picked up on the compassion in the words. It sounded as if Neil had first-hand experience with the fallout of Willow's disappearance. "How about your dad?" she asked softly. "Finding her must've been hard on him."

Neil smiled a crooked smile that didn't reach his eyes. "You were her daughter—nobody was affected more. And still you wonder how my dad was doing?"

"Yes," Jenny murmured. "I can't imagine how it felt to find her out here."

Neil cleared his throat. "He was never the same. I really think he had convinced himself that he would find Willow alive."

Jenny looked at the dog sniffing the leaves of a fern. "She was lost for too long. She died of exposure."

"See, my dad never believed that." Neil sucked in a breath. "Sorry. I have no business startling you and then telling you *that*, of all things." He tugged his dog back. "Come on, Diggory. We should be off."

Jenny put a hand on his arm to keep him back. "Why would your dad not believe it was exposure?"

"I really don't know." Clearly uncomfortable, Neil shrugged his shoulders. "He only talked about it a few times. He thought she should have lived—that there was good water in the creek, and drinking water was the most important thing for survival. Of course that was just his opinion. It's easy to be near the creek and not find it anyway. It's easy to be hydrated and still succumb to the elements."

Jenny nodded. "Unfortunately, that's true." Everyone had their own theories about exactly what had happened to Mom. At first, hearing people talk about it had shocked her. But over the years, she'd gotten to expect it.

Neil straightened his back. "I shouldn't talk of things I don't know anything about."

Jenny glanced at him. "I asked. It's okay. Your dad found her. It's only natural he struggled with the reality of it."

"I'm sure it was his way of hoping there was more of an explanation for such a senseless loss."

"We all searched for that explanation. But sometimes, there isn't one." Jenny took her hand off his arm. "I should get back to my aunt. We'd better wrap up this walk before she's altogether out of energy. She's been getting slower and slower."

Neil ran a hand through his hair and glanced over to Aunt Georgie. "The path gets pretty steep between the creek and the parking lot. Let me walk with you. You might need a hand helping your aunt back up the mountain."

Jenny hesitated. "Um. I think she's pretty shaken, to be honest. She didn't want to come here because of her painful memories. Now your dog reminded her of the one that started the entire terrible chain reaction by breaking free of his collar. Suddenly seeing Diggory gave her such a flashback—it wasn't what I intended for her. I just wanted her to see that the trail is just that. A trail. Nothing to be scared of."

"I agree," Neil said gently. "But the damage is already done. Maybe the best way forward now is for your aunt to walk the dog back herself. Maybe you two should even come to the lighthouse and have a cup of tea with me and Diggory, to cement in her mind that this is a different dog. It might erase the flashback more effectively than leaving now and only remembering the shock of seeing her dog again. What do you think?" He rubbed his chin. "Let's not let our encounter end with shock and fear and bad memories. My dad would never forgive me." He took a deep breath. "*I* would not forgive me."

"If you say it like that..." Jenny tilted her head. "Maybe that's a good idea, actually."

"Jenny? What's going on? What are you two whispering?" Aunt Georgie called out. "Help me up, darling. My knees are sore."

Jenny turned and walked back to the tree trunk. "Listen, Aunt Georgie, Neil here just invited us to visit the lighthouse on Mendocino Island. I would love to go. How about you?"

"The lighthouse? On the island?" Aunt Georgie narrowed her eyes, taking Jenny's hand to haul herself to her feet. Heavier than Jenny had anticipated, her aunt almost pulled her off-balance.

Actually, Neil had an excellent point. It would be good to have his help to get Georgie up the hill.

Jenny waved Neil over, and they exchanged a quick look of understanding. "Let's walk back home together."

Neil smiled at Aunt Georgie. "If you are okay holding Diggory's leash, I'd have an arm for both you and your niece. Holding on to it would make it easier to step over all these roots and rocks."

Aunt Georgie's gaze went to the small dog that was happily panting at her feet. It took her a moment to speak. "Hello, puppy," she then said in a voice Jenny hadn't heard in ages.

Little Diggory looked up at her, grinning widely.

Aunt Georgie took the leash and smiled. "Oh my goodness, look at those dirty paws. Who's a good boy?"

CHAPTER 14

Safely back in the lighthouse, Neil handed Aunt Georgie a big mug. Fragrant steam curled from it, rising to join the old wood beams in the ceiling.

"Thank you, young man." Aunt Georgie took the tea and sat down in a cozy armchair in front of the pretty, if cold, fireplace.

Sunlight streamed through the windows, drawing bright patterns on the wide, wooden planks of the floor. A green vase full of marigolds cheered up the mantel. Jenny wondered whether Neil had picked the flowers himself.

"The tea is hot and sweet and good for the soul." He smiled at Aunt Georgie. "That's what my dad used to say when he stirred in his five spoonfuls of sugar."

"Five spoonfuls is too much," Aunt Georgie said bossily. Walking Diggory had restored her mood. She hadn't even needed Neil's arm to climb the steep part of the trail, walking ahead of him and Jenny most of the time.

"I agree." Neil leaned against the fireplace mantle. "But the fog is thick and cold at night, and the sea wind can nip pretty hard at fingers and toes. Sugary tea is an old sailor trick to stay warm."

"I thought the trick was a good old splash of rum."

"That's another trick. Would you like some?" Neil grinned.

"No, thank you. It's a hot summer day not a foggy night, and I'm not cold at all. What was your dad's name?" Aunt Georgie asked and sipped her tea with pursed lips.

Neil glanced at Jenny. She nodded over her own mug of tea.

"Ray," Neil answered. "His name was Ray Bennett."

"That name..." Aunt Georgie frowned at Diggory, who looked up from his red chewy toy with shiny brown eyes. She reached out and patted his fuzzy little head. "How do I know the name? Did we go to school together?"

"He found Mom in the forest," Jenny whispered. "He was the volunteer fireman who finally found her."

Aunt Georgie lowered her eyes. "Ah yes. That's it. I thought I recognized the name," she murmured.

Neil cleared his throat. "Did you know my dad?"

"No, I didn't know him other than...that." Diggory rolled on his back, offering his pink puppy belly. She petted him briefly but then pulled away her hand and looked up. "He talked to Mom and me afterward. I remember thinking he was too old to be a firefighter."

"He was only a little older than Willow herself," Neil said quietly. "But he barely slept while he was still searching. Maybe that's why he seemed so old to you."

"Your grandpa used to be the lighthouse keeper back when I was a kid." Aunt Georgie abruptly changed the topic. "I remember he ran the ferry, with his gnarly hands and black pirate beard. I saw him sometimes."

"Gramps did enjoy chatting with the people taking his boat," Neil confirmed, his crooked smile a response to the pirate beard comment.

"So what are you planning to do with the lighthouse now that you're back?"

"Repair what's broken, for starters. I'm planning on staying a while since I've nowhere else to be right now." Neil looked around. "Luckily, the place was built to last. The living space is in okay shape. Certainly good enough for me." He patted the fireplace mantle. "I prefer it rustic. Less pressure to keep things pristine."

Jenny smiled. "Have you had time to explore the lighthouse yet?"

"What do you mean, explore?" He shifted his weight.

"You've been gone for a long time. Surely there's some exploring to do?"

Neil looked at her for a moment longer, then went to the bookshelf that was built into the thick wall of the tower. "Like this?" He pulled out a book, cracked it open, and glanced at her through lowered lashes.

She laughed. "Yeah. Like that."

"That's not proper exploring, is it?" Aunt Georgie said. "Exploring is looking in old cupboards and rummaging around the attic."

Jenny smiled at her. "You're right. I stand corrected."

Neil closed the book and returned it to its shelf. "What is it you do, Jenny?"

"I'm an adjunct professor of history at Lizzy May University." She would never grow tired of saying it. The job was more than she'd hoped for when she left Maine with no idea if anyone would hire her after being a stay-at-home mom for so many years. "Mostly, I teach. And I research the lives of my ancestors."

He smiled. "Who were your ancestors?"

"They were whaling families in Nantucket."

His smile deepened. "How staid of them."

Jenny smiled back. "Actually, the ones I happen to research were anything but staid. They eloped, stole a valuable whaler, and sailed themselves to the coast of Mendocino."

"I like them already. I hope they had pirate beards too." Neil pulled out another book, letting it fall open. He looked down at it. "Oh."

"What?" Jenny put down her tea and stood. "Did you find something interesting?"

He frowned. "Looks like Dad wrote this. I didn't know."

"He kept a journal?" Her history sense tingling, Jenny went over to Neil.

"He was always keeping logs and things, but this is a private journal," Neil said, his eyes glued to the pages. Then he looked up, straight into Jenny's eyes, and closed the book. "Jenny, have I shown you the..." His voice trailed off.

She tilted her head. "The...the what?"

"Erm, the lantern room. With the beacon light."

Jenny inhaled to say yes, she had seen it during the tour, when she noticed his gaze slide to Aunt Georgie. She let the breath go without saying the words. He knew she had seen the lantern room.

"No," she said quietly. "But I would like to see it."

He nodded his head toward the door.

"Aunt Georgie?" Jenny turned. "Do you want to come to the top of the tower with me?"

"Heck no." Aunt Georgie patted her lap. Diggory jumped up, turning a couple of times in a tight circle before curling up with a tired sigh. "You two want to talk, and that's none of my business. Go ahead."

It made Jenny chuckle. Whatever Aunt Georgie's problems were, being slow on the uptake wasn't among them. "Just a quick glance. I'll be back soon."

"Sure." Aunt Georgie's eyes were fixed on the fireplace. "Don't do anything I wouldn't do." She sighed. "Or rather, don't do *that*."

"I'll be a good girl—within reasonable limits." Jenny went over to her and pressed a kiss on the top of her aunt's head. It was a risky venture to get this affectionate with her brambly relative, but Georgie didn't even flinch.

Neil opened the door and let Jenny go first. Feeling his eyes on her back, she started climbing the sturdy stairs.

The air in the large, round room was warm, heated by the afternoon sun streaming in through all the windows. Neil cracked open one of them, letting in fresh air and the rushing of the Pacific that shimmered like a precious, azure jewel below the summery bluff. Jenny joined Neil at the window. "It's so beautiful. If this were my house, I'd sit up here all the time."

"Over there." Neil pointed at two ancient Chesterfield armchairs with deep button tufting, rolled arms, and tan leather upholstery looking buttery soft with old age. They stood facing the sea and the cove and the sky. Smudges on the whitewashed window ledge before one of the chairs showed that Neil liked to put his feet up.

He looked from Jenny to the smudges and back. "That was Dad. Or maybe Gramps. I'm a modern man. I take my shoes off."

"I wasn't going to say anything." Again, Jenny had to smile. Something about Neil made her happy. It wasn't every day she met guys like him. "I guess you have more pressing worries than painting. The glass needs replacing soon, doesn't it?" She touched the glass in the next panel. Clearly antique, it was so thick and warped that the view was distorted.

"That's a lens, actually, and I'm pretty sure it'll outlast the chairs. But you have to look at it from over here."

"A lens?" Jenny stepped where he indicated and peered through the glass. The view was magnified, as if it wasn't beautiful enough already.

"Yep. It's called a Fresnel lens, since you're asking, and it's specially made to focus the beacon. Its prisms bend light to make a powerful beam that can be seen far away."

Slowly, Jenny turned on her heel. "There are alternating sections of normal glass and prisms."

"Now you know enough to become the next lighthouse keeper."

"I always wanted to be one." Jenny turned back to Neil, finding his eyes on her. "But that ship has sailed. Let's talk about the book you found."

"Right." Neil set the book on the window ledge. "It's my dad's journal. It fell open to a newspaper clipping."

Jenny crossed her arms. She had a feeling she knew what the clipping was about. "My mom?"

"Yes, your mom." Neil opened the book and handed Jenny the clipping.

She took it and read only the first few lines before handing it back. "He found her. They mention his name. I think it's easy to understand why he kept the clip."

"There's more." Neil ran a hand along his jaw. "Listen, let's sit down for a moment. I didn't have time to read it all downstairs, and I didn't want your aunt to ask. Let's sit in the chairs."

The hairs on Jenny's neck stood up. "We can't take long," she murmured and went to sit. The chair really was buttery soft, but she couldn't appreciate it. "It's never a good idea to let my aunt get bored."

"Erm." Neil sat beside her, eyes skipping along the lines of the journal entries on the open page. "Dad writes here that your mom died of a snake bite," he said without further preamble.

Jenny looked down at the book on his knees. "A snake bite?"

"I'm sorry." Neil flipped the page. "I'm only letting you know because I saw he had this." He pulled out another folded piece of paper and opened it. "It's a toxicology report."

"A toxicology report?" Jenny pulled her chin back. "There was a toxicology report?"

Neil glanced at her. "Your grandmother must have gotten a copy, no? She didn't tell you?"

"No. Nobody told me anything. They just shipped me off to Nantucket."

"Maybe she never did get the report? It's possible she would have had to specially request a copy. I don't know how exactly it worked back then."

Jenny put a hand to her forehead. Whatever Grandma Rosie did or didn't share with her—why on earth did Neil's dad have a copy? He wasn't family. She dropped her hand again. "*I* should've had one. It never occurred to me to ask for a toxicology report. I should have written and asked about it ages ago."

Neil's eyes flew over the report. "They don't exactly teach that stuff in school, and you were just a kid. Anyway, it wouldn't have made a difference. They didn't find anything. No obvious venom. And nothing else, either." He folded the report again and tucked it back into the book, shaking his head. "I'm sorry if I scared you, Jenny, bringing you up here. Dad must have asked for this report to check on his snake bite hypothesis."

Jenny fell back into her chair. "Does your dad write in his journal *why* he was so convinced it was a snake bite?"

"Do you want to read it yourself?"

She shook her head. "It wasn't written for me. You have a look."

"Hmm." Neil turned another page. "He found a shed snakeskin near the root. I think that's maybe all the evidence he had."

"It's not much."

"No, it really isn't. Rattlesnakes are not likely to bite unless they get stepped on—and they try to stay away from people. Plus, the report shows Willow wasn't bitten." Neil closed the journal and scrambled to his feet. "I'm an idiot. Let's go back down."

Jenny inhaled, held the breath for a moment, and then let it go with a whoosh. "Why did your dad order a copy of the report?"

Neil shrugged. "He never mentioned it to me. I know he had a friend who worked for the coroner; maybe that's how he got it? But it doesn't matter. I should've read it before upsetting you for nothing."

Jenny bit her lip, reminding herself that finding her mom had affected Ray deeply and that it was natural for people to try to find out what happened. "It's okay. I like that you let me know right away."

Neil held out a hand, and Jenny took it, letting him pull her up. "Oops." He'd pulled too hard, and she stumbled into his arms.

With any other man—apart from Jon—she'd have immediately stepped back.

But she liked Neil.

Wrapping her arms around his neck felt good.

Jenny buried her face on his shoulder, and for a few heartbeats, Neil held her in his arms.

Then he murmured, "Maybe we really should go back down to your aunt."

"Yes." Jenny dropped her arms and stepped back. The hug had made her feel better. Safer and warm. "Let's go down."

This time, Neil led the way, and Jenny followed.

Aunt Georgie was still sitting in the cozy living room, empty tea mug in hands, eyes unseeingly staring at the fireplace. Diggory was happily ripping apart a stuffed toy by her feet. Sometimes, he bit on the squeaker and perked his ears at the silly sound.

"Everything okay?" Jenny said lightly and took the mug from her aunt.

"Darling," Aunt Georgie murmured and blinked. "Was it nice?"

"Was what nice?"

Aunt Georgie circled her hand in a gesture as vague as her voice. "The thing. The room."

"Oh. Very much. The view is stunning up there."

Neil lifted the big, brown teapot. "More tea?"

"No." With a small groan, Aunt Georgie bent down and patted the little dog, who wagged a friendly acknowledgment of the attention. "We should leave, Jenny. I have things to do."

"Yes." Jenny held out a hand to help her aunt up. "Let's go home."

Neil put his teapot back on the table. "Unless you want a tour of the lower lighthouse first, Miss Summers? Jenny has seen the place, but you missed the lantern tour."

Jenny turned to her aunt. "And the view from the lantern room *is* spectacular. Also a lot of steps, though."

"For now, I'll be grateful to get down the ones we climbed already. My joints fell asleep while you were gone." Aunt Georgie huffed and rose stiffly. Not even twenty years separated her and Jenny, but they did make a difference.

"We'll take it nice and slow," Jenny promised. "We can always just catch the next ferry. No need to hurry."

"There's a dance at the lighthouse tomorrow," Neil said. "It's just outside in the old garden—or what's left of the old garden. I still have to set up a wooden floor. Nothing big, but it would be nice to see you two again."

Jenny smiled. "Oh, that's right. Billie texted me about the dance. What do you think, Aunt Georgie?"

"Why not? As long as you keep that dog of yours safe inside."

"Diggory will be sleeping soundly on the sofa by the fireplace," Neil promised. "You can join him anytime if you get tired." He helped Aunt Georgie downstairs and opened the door.

Aunt Georgie stepped outside. With a dramatic sigh, she sank onto a bench by the door, turned her face in the sun, and closed her eyes. "Just a moment to catch my breath, darlings. I'm not used to so much exercise."

"Sure. Take your time." Jenny sat beside her. "We've already done most of the walking for today. We only have to get back to the ferry. Our car is waiting for us on the other side."

Neil closed the front door. "I hope you know I'm more than happy to drive you to the ferry."

Each way, the ferry could accommodate up to two cars along with the passengers. The island and the cove had a silent understanding that, whenever possible, the scarce car spots were given to the islanders, who in turn offered their friendly neighbors rides back to the ferry. In that spirit, Neil had brought his car back to the island while Jenny and Aunt Georgie left their own car parked on the cove side and hitched a ride to get from the small harbor to the lighthouse.

"Should we take him up on the offer?" Jenny asked her aunt.

"Thanks, darling, but no." Aunt Georgie's eyes fluttered open as she mustered the strength to rise to her feet. "You've done enough," she declared once she succeeded.

Neil glanced at Jenny, who nodded. If Aunt Georgie wanted to walk, they walked.

"Right. Bye then." Abruptly, Neil turned and went to the crooked wooden fence surrounding the wild garden to look out at the sea.

"Bye," Jenny said quietly and offered her aunt her arm. "Did you just call the island's new lighthouse keeper *darling*?" she whispered when they stepped onto the narrow path leading to the harbor.

"Did I?" Aunt Georgie walked surprisingly fast for being old and exhausted. "I wasn't paying attention. But so what if I did? Isn't he?"

Jenny raised an eyebrow and glanced over. "Isn't he what?"

"Darling. Isn't he a darling?" Her aunt's eyes on her were as surprisingly sharp as her walk was quick.

"Yes." Jenny had to hurry to keep up. "I think maybe he is."

CHAPTER 15

I s the dress too much? I can't tell." Billie tugged on
the sleeve. She'd had the dress for ages because
she'd fallen in love with it at first sight, but this night
was the first time she ever put it on. "It's too much, isn't
it?"

"It's a bit late to change, Billie," Ava said mildly.

The friends were standing on the upstairs outdoor
seating deck of the ferry, letting their fancy skirts flutter
in the wind. Audrey and Aunt Georgie had elected to
stay downstairs inside the cabin, and the men were
already at the lighthouse, helping Neil set up the dance
floor for the fundraising event.

"That's hardly helpful, Ava," Billie complained. She
should have gone in a simple summer dress, the kind
she wore to the market any old day.

"I—" A gust of wind lifted the skirt of her straight,
tea-length Charleston dress of champagne satin, and
she turned to avoid the gust with a few choice, unlady-
like expressions.

"Billie, your dress is great. So are ours." Faye pushed
a long curl back into her updo. "Who cares whether
they're too much? We're at an age where we should

wear whatever we want. And you do look beautiful. Like a water nymph."

"A *water* nymph? A water *nymph?*" Billie spread her arms and looked down at her dress. "Is that a compliment, or nah, or...?"

"Definitely a compliment," Faye reassured her. "I've always wanted to see one. And ta-daa—along came your fabulous self in this spirited masterpiece."

"Hmm." Billie didn't see herself as a nymph of any description. Hopefully, Faye meant what she said about it being a compliment. When she looked up to inspect her friend's face, Billie pulled her chin back. "Hey, Faye—are you okay?"

"I think I'm going to throw up. Only I can't tell if it's morning sickness or motion sickness." Faye suddenly held a hand to her mouth. "Ugh! Is this ever going to get better? I'm sick and tired of being sick and tired."

The image made Billie smile because Faye wore a floor-length gown in deep emerald green, with an off-the-shoulder neckline that swooped into a subtle empire waist and a cascading skirt to hide her baby bump. She claimed the bump had managed to grow visibly in the last few days.

"I'm so sorry, Faye. It will get better. I promise. Give it plus minus eighteen years." Ava had rearranged her own skirt and turned back to them. "And Billie, you're a vision of elegance with that dreamy, ethereal silhouette. I swear on my mother's grave."

"Am I really?" Billie wanted to look good for the dance. Everyone would be there, and if she really was so important for representing the cove as her brother and cousins claimed, she should look pulled together.

Ava nodded. "My jaw literally dropped when I saw you. I mean, I knew about those curves, but where does that tiny little waist come from all of a sudden? Is that from cleaning out the pelican enclosures? All that bending and twisting?"

Billie's hand went to the bodice, her fingers feeling the delicate lace and the subtle sequins that twinkled like stars on the soft blue fabric.

"Aww. Ethereal? Really? Thank you. Ethereal is way better than water nymph, isn't it?"

"No," Faye said. "Nothing's better than that."

"Billie's waist has always been there, hidden under all those wide shirts and flannel," Jenny chimed in. "I've told her a hundred times to show it off." Jenny wore the least formal dress—knee-length, in a playful, cheerful floral print of coral, mint, and lemon, which she'd paired with a green velvet belt and dainty gold jewelry.

"Wide shirts and flannels are comfy, and nobody cares about my measurements," Billie said, but the words got swallowed by the huffing of the engine as the ferry slowed to approach the island harbor.

Billie gathered the fluttering skirt that cascaded in waves from her waist to the floor. "Here we go," she called to her friends. "You think we'll be early?"

"We were supposed to be much earlier than this!" Jenny called back over the noise of the pumping pistons.

Clutching railings and posts to steady themselves, they made their way to the metal staircase leading downstairs. Hitching their skirts high, they descended the stairs, and in a flurry of fabric and pearls, sequins and heels, they stepped off the boat and onto the island.

"Thank heavens. I don't know that I would've held on much longer." Faye looked relieved to have firm ground under her feet again.

"Oh, it's going to be so fun. I've not been dancing in... I can't even remember." Jenny shook her blonde curls back and lifted her colorful skirt.

"My party," Ava said pointedly. "You danced at my recommitment ceremony. It's not long ago at all."

"Mom?" Audrey came toward their group, her great-aunt in tow. "We're going to catch a ride, okay? Meet you at the lighthouse."

"Sure, sweetheart."

"Are you sure that man is to be trusted, child?" Georgie asked and looked at a person waiting nearby.

"Yes. His name is Thomas, and he's the mailman. I've told you twice already, Auntie." Audrey sounded mildly exasperated, as if the ride with her aunt had tested her nerves.

Georgie raised her eyebrows. "Don't call me Auntie! That sounds weird. I'm your great-aunt, not your auntie, child."

"And *I'm* your great-niece, not a child. You call me great-niece, and I'll call you great-aunt. I also have a name, you know."

Bickering, the two left to take advantage of the offered ride with Tommy, the island's mail carrier.

"It's dark enough that nobody is going to see the dust on the dresses," Ava said as the car left. She shimmied a few steps up the sandy lane leading to the lighthouse, making the fringe on her dress swing and glitter in the sun. "Come on, gals. We've been looking forward to this. We don't want to miss a good summer dance."

"Speak for yourself. I'm only going because Jon and Lex made me." Billie lifted her flowing skirt so it wouldn't trail in the dust and followed her friends.

The island was never more beautiful than when the sun set over the rugged coastline, bathing sea and land in gold and fire. The bluff, warmed by a long, hot, dry summer, smelled of sweet herbs and wildflowers, grasses and coastal shrubs. The ever-present ocean added its salty tang to the perfume, and now and then, there was a whiff of a distant beach bonfire.

The breeze played with their hair and skirts as they walked along, chatting about Ava's house renovations and Faye's new ultrasound images that showed a perfectly healthy baby and had found a permanent home in the proud father's wallet. Following the sound of soft music in the air, they soon reached the wild garden surrounding the lighthouse.

Jenny stopped short, her eyes widening with pleasure. "Will you look at that?"

In the dusky light, the overgrown flowerbeds had turned into a whimsical oasis of daisies, roses, and lavender, mingling together in a riot of colors and sweet scents. Twinkling fairy lights were strung between the trees, casting a soft, romantic glow that illuminated a large, circular wooden dance floor.

The men had set it up only a few steps away from the lighthouse, positioning it to offer breathtaking views of the crashing waves below the bluff. Woven wicker baskets filled with more flowers and bottles of water and soda gave it a charming touch. Delicate, pastel paper lanterns with hand-painted marine motives were strung between tall posts in the corners of the floor, adding a magical ambiance as they flickered with soft, electric candlelight. A small band was playing already, and people, their faces excited and happy, milled around.

Billie closed her mouth. "When did they even have time to do all that? It's like a wedding! Now I'm glad I pulled out all the stops and put up my hair."

"Your hair is too short to put up," Faye whispered, awed. "It's so pretty! Look at the lanterns... That one has lobsters on it! Cute!"

"I *love* the tables!" Ava clasped her hands like a child at Christmas.

Tables draped in crisp white linen were scattered around the dance floor, each decorated with centerpieces made of seashells, starfish, and even more blossoms.

"Here—step aside," Jenny warned.

A car drove up to the lighthouse, then another, and more guests spilled out. The women had donned flowing dresses in shades ranging from bold to pastel, while men wore linen slacks or suits paired with open-collared shirts. Many people wore delicate flower crowns or boutonnieres crafted from the island gardens' blooms that seemed to get handed out at one of the long buffet tables.

"Billie? You look stunning. Hi, Faye. Ava—Jenny." An old school friend had spotted them and hugged them one after the other. "Here." She threaded flower crowns off her arm and showed them. "Will you buy one? All profits go to the lighthouse renovation. Specifically, the beacon—we islanders want to see it light up again."

"So do we Covians. Four crowns, please." Ava fished money from her silk pouch and handed each of her friends a flower crown.

Billie took hers and pressed it on her head. "I had no idea we could make things to sell," she mumbled. "If Neil would've said anything, I would've baked something." She always pitched in—it was weird not to be included in the fundraising part.

"We look good." Jenny pulled out her cell phone, waving to the friend who was moving on to sell more crowns. "Huddle together, girls. Selfie time."

Billie obliged, surreptitiously eyeing the crowd. Jon and Lex had given Billie the impression that she was needed for the cove's body count. Now it turned out that scenario was far from reality. When the band struck up a popular new song, all of Mendocino Cove seemed to stream onto the wooden dance floor.

"Welcome to the lighthouse dance! This way, ladies!" someone shouted.

"There they are!" Jenny pointed and started walking.

At the rickety gate of the crooked fence stood Jon, Lex, and Gabe. Jenny raised onto her tiptoes and pressed a kiss on Jon's cheek. Putting an arm around her shoulders, Jon leaned down and kissed her back on the lips. Gabe went straight to his pregnant soon-to-be wife, and Ava had already swerved away from them to meet Bruno, her longtime husband, who was waving at her from the far side of the dancers.

"And just like that, they were gone," Billie murmured to herself and walked to the buffet table all by her lonesome.

CHAPTER 16

Watching the crowd, Billie bit into a churro. It melted in her mouth, and the warm cinnamon sugar was a decent substitute for having friends who actually stuck with you.

Oh. There was one of them, approaching from the right.

Billie smiled tentatively.

"Neil gave a good speech, didn't he?" Ava asked and smiled back. Eyes beaming with happiness, she was still hanging on to Bruno's arm.

"Sure did." Billie swallowed her treat and dusted sugar off her hands.

"It was heartwarming." Bruno stopped.

"It was," Billie agreed. Neil had expressed gratitude for the support of everyone who'd shown up and highlighted the importance of preserving the historic lighthouse. Nothing wrong with that, as far as Billie could tell.

"They're playing our song," Bruno said. "Do you want to dance, my dear?"

"You know I do." Ava's eyes turned an even deeper shade of happy as she gazed at her husband.

"Have fun, you two." Billie picked up another churro from the platter beside her. Whoever had made them knew what they were doing.

"Did you buy any raffle tickets?" Faye asked, coming from the left with Gabe, who surveyed the crowd as if he was security, not a guest.

Billie breathed in cinnamon sugar and coughed. "Goodness, Faye, you startled me."

"So did you?" her friend demanded.

"Yes. I bought twenty tickets. Good?"

Faye nodded, satisfied, then looked around. "Why are you all alone? Do you want company? We can sit down, if you like." She peered at the dance floor from under her lashes, her fingers tapping her thigh in rhythm to the band's cheerful melody.

"Nah. I want to stand here and eat churros." Billie picked up another long, toasty-brown confection and pointed it at Gabe. "Take her away, please."

"You got it, Billie." Gabe winked, put an arm around his fiancée's waist, and pulled Faye, who was inhaling to say more, toward the music.

"Hey. Billie. Did you dance with Neil yet?" Now it was Jon who came to stand by her.

Billie sighed and set the churro on a napkin.

"You have cinnamon on you...there." Her brother pointed.

Billie wiped her lips. "No. I have not."

Jon raised an eyebrow. "Why not? You said you would. In fact, you promised."

"Jon, really?" Billie raised her free hand accusingly. "You and Lex made it sound like Neil had trouble getting people to come. Look around! It's so full I can't even... The entire island is here. And so is the cove."

"I know." Jon surveyed the crowd with a satisfied expression. "I told you he belongs to an old island family. People remember."

Billie picked her churro back up. "So, he doesn't need me. I'm good here, eating my way through the desserts."

Jon turned to her. "Look at you."

Billie looked down at herself. "What?"

"Stop eating to while away the time." He took the churro from her and bit into it. "You look beautiful. What are you doing, standing here by yourself?"

Billie frowned and licked powdered sugar from her thumb. "Where's Jenny?"

"Dancing with Neil, actually."

Billie craned her neck, but there were too many people on the dance floor. She couldn't spot Jenny. "Um. Are you sure that's a good idea?"

"Again with the suspicions?" Jon shook his head. "Come on, Bills. Jenny likes Neil, but she also likes Bruno, Gabe, and Lex. It's fine."

"Okay." Billie turned to pick up another churro, but they were all gone. A woman across the table was holding the last one and threw her an apologetic look. Billie nodded—she'd eaten enough, anyway.

Beside her, Jon tensed. "Uh-oh. Billie, Ian's coming over here. I'm out. Bye."

"Jon!" Billie hissed. "Stay!"

But her brother had already vanished into the crowd.

"Billie! Listen," Ian called out busily, scarcely in talking distance yet and flashing smiles at the people he was passing.

"Hi, Ian. Are we back on speaking terms?" Billie crossed her arms. Last time they met, he had stormed dramatically out of the Mermaid Galley, leaving her to pay for his cocktail.

Ian lunged into the crowd and pulled out a pretty, middle-aged woman. "Billie!"

"Still my name." Billie pressed her lips together.

Ian reached her, pulling the pretty woman with him. She looked put out, with a line growing between her finely drawn eyebrows. "This is Francesca."

"Oh." Billie had never met his paramour. "Right. Hi."

"Hi." Francesca blinked. In her hands, she awkwardly held two churros, loosely wrapped in a napkin. "Hi, Billie."

"I wanted you two to finally meet," Ian said boisterously. "It's about time, don't you think?"

Billie did her best to smile. "Sure. Nice to meet you, Francesca," she said politely.

"Nice to meet you too." Francesca smiled back.

"Excuse me?" Someone tapped Ian on the shoulder. "Aren't you the guy who directed *I, Liberation*? I love your work!"

"Thank you! Thank you very much!" Ian turned to his fan, leaving the two women to their own devices.

They looked at each other. Finally, Francesca inhaled. "Billie—I've wanted to talk with you for the longest time."

"You have?" Billie dropped her arms. Now she wished she'd gone dancing after all.

Francesca nodded. Her lush black hair fell over her shoulder, and she pushed it back gracefully. "But if you'd rather not, I understand. I'll leave you alone."

"No, it's fine." Billie leaned against the table. "Maybe we should talk. Especially if you and Ian are going to be my new neighbors."

"I, um... I want to apologize." Francesca's liquid eyes met Billie's. "For...back then."

Billie didn't know what to do with that. "You don't have to do that. As far as I'm concerned, it was Ian's decision to cheat on the mother of his sons."

Francesca bit her lip. "It probably doesn't make a difference, but...I didn't know Ian was married when he asked me out."

"No?" Billie tilted her head. "Is that right?"

"Well..." Francesca hesitated. "I suppose I could have found out. I should have asked around. But I didn't do that—and he never mentioned it. I promise."

Something in Billie relented. "It wasn't your responsibility to find out what all he wasn't telling you. Don't worry about it. I'm thoroughly over Ian."

"I know." Francesca looked down at her hands. "But I was hoping... I was hoping you could forgive me. When I finally heard that he was married with kids, I broke up with him. Only..."

Billie smiled. "Only it was true love?"

Francesca smiled back. "Sort of. We have a long history of separating and getting back together." She sighed. "Honestly, he's a prat and an adulterer, but I'm no saint either. And I do love him. This last time we got back together, something clicked. Now it's different for us. We're ready to take the jump."

Behind them, Ian laughed—too loud, too long—at something his fan had said.

"Good for you." Billie waited until Ian was done so she could be heard. "I also thought I was in love with him, and he left me hurt and disillusioned. But honestly, I'd have divorced him one way or the other. His unfaithfulness saved me from what would otherwise have been the long, inevitable decline of our marriage. It was hard when the boys were little, but I have a large family that helped me out."

"That's a relief." Francesca took a big breath. "Ian's not an easy person. We've been through a lot over the years. But somehow, we always find each other again." Francesca turned to him, and Billie caught the look her ex and his beloved exchanged. There was silent communication and understanding, something she and Ian had never shared.

"Good," Billie said, surprising herself with how genuinely she meant it. "I'm glad for you two." For a brief moment, Billie had believed she and Ian could spark something again. But she'd been wrong, and it hadn't taken her long to figure it out.

Francesca turned back to her, and her smile deepened. "You don't have to be, you know. I'm not asking that much—just that we be civil. I'd like to say hi in the market, and I was hoping we wouldn't have to change sidewalks in town when we meet. That sort of thing."

Behind Francesca, Billie spotted Faye and Jenny's faces, their eyes asking whether she needed help. Her friends had analyzed the situation and were ready to move in if need be. Smiling, Billie shook her head, half at her friends having her back after all, half at Francesca's vision of their life as neighbors. "Of course we're not changing sidewalks when we see each other," Billie said. "Don't be silly. The town would stage an intervention if we did. It would be so awkward sitting there and having the major scold us while all the fishermen shuffle their feet in the back, waiting their turn to talk. Though I'm pretty sure my neighbor would bring lemon cake. But we can get that for the asking."

Francesca's smile reached her eyes. "Oof." She exhaled. "I'm so glad," she said with a little laugh. "I'm so glad you and I are all right, Billie."

"We definitely are."

"If you don't mind my asking... Do you have someone?" Francesca tilted her head.

"I don't have a partner if that's what you're thinking of. I'm the odd one out."

"Odd one out? What do you mean?"

"Oh." Billie cleared her throat. "My friends. They've all found their one true love." It felt stupid to say it out loud.

"I'm sorry." Francesca frowned. Then she held out the napkin with the last two churros. "Do you want to have a churro?"

For a moment, Billie looked at the treat. Then she took one. "Thanks."

"Sure." Francesca bit into hers. "Hey, these are good."

"Aren't they?"

"We have similar tastes." Francesca's smile bordered on impish, but her eyes were seeking Billie's permission.

"Hmm." Billie couldn't really laugh, but she managed a chuckle. "I suppose so."

Encouraged, Francesca came to lean against the table beside Billie. "What about him?" She pointed with her chin at someone in the crowd. "He looks nice."

"Who do you—oh. That's Neil." Billie finished her treat and wiped her fingers on a napkin. "Um, no."

As if he could feel their eyes on him, Neil turned his head and looked at Billie.

Francesca finished her churro and pushed off the table. "I'll see you around, Billie." She wiped her hand on a napkin and held it out. "It was really nice talking to you. Thank you."

"No worries." Billie wiped her hand too and shook. "I'll see you around town."

Smiling, Francesca left.

Brushing cinnamon sugar off her dress, Billie straightened. She glanced at Neil. He was close enough to have heard what they were saying. Hopefully, he hadn't listened in. She shouldn't have said *no* to Francesca's suggestion quite so emphatically.

Neil looked at the ground, but then he walked over to her. "You came," he said. He was wearing a suit but had taken off the jacket and rolled up his sleeves.

Billie looked up, meeting his eyes. "I did. I thought I should support my island neighbors. Well, you. I guess that's only one neighbor. Though of course I support the other ones as well. Just in general. But also...specifically? Uh—what?" She took a deep breath, noticing too late how it swelled her exposed décolletage. Quickly, she exhaled to deflate.

"That's good of you, Billie. Erm. You have something..." With a finger, he flicked something off Billie's face. "Sugar?" He smiled.

"The churros," Billie admitted sheepishly, wiping her cheek with the back of her hand. "They were so good. I wish I knew who made them so I can ask for the recipe."

"I made them. The recipe is a secret."

Billie tilted her head. "Why is it a secret?"

The music changed to a new song, and Neil offered his hand. It took Billie a moment to understand what he wanted, but then she put her hand in his. His fingers felt warm, and strong, and effortlessly and entirely closed around hers.

"Because," Neil said while leading her to the dance floor, "I had to travel seven seas to find it. It can't be had simply for the asking."

He put Billie's hand on his shoulder, his own on her waist, and pulled her close.

Billie's eyelashes fluttered involuntarily. She blew out a small, tense breath through pursed lips, glad she was too close to his chest for him to see her face.

"What is it?" Slowly, Neil started dancing, expertly moving her with him.

"Oh. Nothing." Billie tried to focus on her feet and the steps her mother had taught her, not the manly chest radiating heat onto her cheeks. Luckily, she remembered enough not to make a fool of herself.

"Listen to that," Neil murmured.

"The music?"

"That, too. But I mean the people. The sea. The night."

Billie listened. Laughter and chatter filled the air as friends and neighbors celebrated the lighthouse on Mendocino Island. The sounds of cicadas and katydids made the night air shimmer, and the faint crashing of waves could be heard below the bluff.

The night sounded magical, breathtaking, effortlessly enchanted in the way nights at the coast always sounded when one listened close enough.

"It's nice," was all Billie could think to say.

"I feel like we got off on the wrong foot, last time we met," Neil said and twirled Billie around.

"That is possible," she said when she was back in his arms.

Maybe it had been Francesca's bravery when she came to talk that put Billie in a softer, gentler mood. Maybe it had been Jon and Lex declaring that Neil was a friend, or maybe it was nothing more than the golden moon and stars rising into the deep-blue velvet of the night.

"I meant to tell you something, Billie," Neil murmured.

CHAPTER 17

"What do you want to tell me?" Billie asked.

Neil lifted his arm. Billie turned again without missing a beat, her skirt twirling a wide circle. He smiled. "I meant to tell you that your dress is beautiful. *You* are beautiful."

"Oh! Oh." Hot blood shot into Billie's cheeks. "Um. Thanks."

He didn't say anything more, and when the music slowed, he let her go. "Thank you for the dance, Billie. Listen, I'd better go talk to the mayor before she leaves."

Billie would have liked to see the color of his irises. But despite the bright stars, the glowing lanterns and flickering torches, his eyes were veiled, and she couldn't make it out.

"Sure," she said. "Thanks for the... um..." She gestured at the dance floor.

"You too, Billie." He nodded and left, waving at the mayor.

Billie looked around.

Now that it was dark, many of the people with children were leaving. The crowd thinned, and as the buzz quieted, the atmosphere changed. Silent moonlight poured silver onto the flowers in the wild garden, and long chains of fairy lights twinkled to life at the base of the lighthouse.

"Hey, Bills." Jon and Jenny, arm in arm, appeared beside Billie. She hadn't noticed them coming over.

"Hey," she said, startled out of her thoughts.

"You look different." Jenny lifted her head off Jon's shoulder to survey her critically. "Are you okay?"

Billie rubbed her arms. Suddenly, the night air felt cool. "I *feel* different," she said and then added, without meaning to, "I finally met Francesca. We talked."

"Did you really?" Jenny asked while Jon took off his jacket.

"Here." He handed it to Billie. "You're cold."

"Thanks." She hung it over her shoulders.

Jenny smiled. "You looked good dancing, Billie. Very graceful."

Billie pulled the jacket close. She'd gotten warm in Neil's arms and was quickly cooling down. "Thanks. Surprisingly, I enjoyed dancing again."

Jon winked. "Not as horrible an experience as you anticipated then?"

"No." Billie grinned sheepishly. "I can't say it was horrible."

Jon and Jenny exchanged a satisfied glance. Billie looked away, trying not to think about the meaning of it. "I'd like to go home," she said. "I want a fire and a cup of sweet milk tea. How is everyone doing?" Since they'd driven to the ferry together, they had planned to leave together too.

"I'm not sure Ava is ready to leave," Jenny said and craned her neck to find their friend in the midst of the dancers. "Faye's still dancing, too."

"Aww, come on, Billie." Jon looked disappointed. "It's early yet. Dance with someone else?"

She shook her head. "It's okay, you guys take the car. I'll call an Uber. I'm tired." There were no Ubers or taxis to be had in the cove at this time of night, but she could just walk home. Nothing was very far in Mendocino Cove.

Jon looked at Jenny, clearly aware of the transport shortage, and Billie inhaled to declare she didn't need her brother to bring her home when a deep voice interrupted her.

"I'll bring you home." Neil had made his way back to them. "I parked a car on the cove side earlier so I can drive people home."

"Oh," Billie said. Her heart jumped a little—she hadn't realized he was so close. "That's all right. Thanks." She didn't need anyone bringing her home.

"No problem," Neil said, clearly thinking she had agreed to his offer. "Jon?"

Her brother nodded. "Thanks, Neil. I'll make sure things go smoothly while you're gone. See you, Billie. Sleep well, ey?" With a grin, Jon took his jacket off Billie.

"She's going to get cold." Neil slipped off his own jacket and put it over Billie's shoulders. His jacket was warmer than Jon's, and it smelled better too.

"Okay?" Neil asked. "I don't want you to catch a cold."

"Okay." Billie smiled at him. "Thanks."

He smiled back.

When Billie looked around again, Jon and Jenny were gone.

"Let's go before someone else wants to chat." Neil lightly put a palm on Billie's lower back, guiding her through the garden and out the gate, releasing his touch only once they were walking down the sandy lane leading to the harbor.

The singing insects and crashing waves filled the night now that the music ebbed behind them, and the moon grew brighter without the fairy lights and torches.

"Are you all right?" Neil asked after walking silently by her side. "I know your ex-husband and his fiancée came tonight. I tried to... Erm, I tried to finagle things to keep him away, but he's pretty oblivious to hints."

Billie glanced up at Neil. "He is. But it's fine—you didn't have to do that."

"Are you two on good terms? I saw you talking to him."

Billie picked a beach daisy as she considered the question. "I don't know if I would call it good terms. I'm on *functional* terms with Ian. We get along, and of course we have the boys together. But Francesca—that's different. I just met her tonight."

"Hmm? How did you feel about her?"

Billie smiled at his interest. "Honestly, I think the two of us will work out well enough. If they really move to the cove... It'll be all right. Maybe it will even be good."

"You're a generous person," Neil said after a while. "I like that."

Billie's heart drummed a little faster. "Neil?" she asked tentatively.

"Yes?"

"I'm sorry I was prickly the first time we met. I thought..." She shook her head at herself. "I thought you showed too much interest in Jenny. She's dating my brother, and..."

"And?" Neil asked softly.

"And Jon's been in love with Jenny forever. She's finally come back to the cove, and I couldn't stand it if she..." Now, she had to laugh at herself. "It sounds so stupid, but I couldn't stand it if she'd left him for another man."

"Left *Jon?*" He sounded amused too. "Your Jenny? I don't think so."

"No, I don't think so either. Not anymore. I just wasn't sure for a hot second."

He chuckled. "I didn't mean to give the impression. She's nice. I like her."

"Mm-hmm." Billie would have liked to ask if Neil liked her the way he liked Jenny. But it felt...risky. Something deep in her belly knew it wasn't that easy. And maybe, Neil would stop in the middle of the empty, moonlit lane, and he would look at her, and...

She exhaled a quiet breath.

It was probably only her overactive imagination.

But just in case. Billie's last relationship was a *very* long time ago, and she wasn't going to stand in a ballroom gown on a moonlit lane on a bluff over the glittering sea, gazing into a handsome lighthouse keeper's eyes. Not Neil's. Not any lighthouse keeper's.

At least not without a lot more mental preparation.

She sped up her walk, looking straight ahead. "I like Jenny too. She's one of my best friends."

He hummed agreement, easily keeping pace.

By the time they reached the harbor, the street lanterns had flickered to life, and the night wind had grown from cool to cold. Islanders out on evening strolls put on sweaters and shawls as they sampled the restaurant menus and admired the pretty shop windows lining the waterfront.

Billie pulled out her phone to check the time. They had just missed the ferry, and the next one was still out half an hour. "You really don't have to wait here with me, Neil," she said. "I'm sure your guests want you back at the lighthouse."

Neil smiled mildly, as if the suggestion he leave her alone at the ferry dock was a weak joke. "What do you think about a coffee before heading back home?"

"Uh..." Billie was stuffed full of churros and the other delicacies offered at the large buffet. "A coffee would be nice," she admitted.

"There's a new café near the ferry dock I think looks promising. We could try it out." Neil nodded down the lantern-lit quay. More people were milling around here, sitting on the benches along the seawall as they waited for the ferry or simply enjoyed the nightly ocean view.

Billie hesitated. "Are you sure you don't want to go back? I can wait for the ferry in the coffee place. I have a ton of books on my phone."

He smiled. "I have time for a hot drink if you do."

"You know I do." Billie couldn't help but smile back.

They soon found the place Neil was looking for. Warm yellow light created a cozy atmosphere as they stepped inside. The smell of freshly brewed coffee filled their noses while soft instrumental music played in the background.

Billie's eyes lit up as she took in her surroundings—the quaint wooden tables and chairs, the whitewashed walls adorned with vintage photos of boats sailing on calm seas. This place was a lovely new addition to the harbor.

Neil ordered two cappuccinos and some pastries while Billie chose a slice of lemon meringue tart for herself. As they waited for their order to arrive, Neil asked Billie about her life back in town. "Tell me about yourself," he said.

"Where to start?" She smoothed her long skirt.

"You have two sons?"

"I do. Louis and Benjamin. Louis is finishing grad school in San Francisco. Ben, the older one, is a vet in Maple Creek."

Neil nodded. "So they're grown men."

Billie smiled. "Sort of."

"Do they visit you often?"

"Sometimes. It's hard for them to get away. Especially Ben, who has a lot of clients at the clinic. Louis can work anywhere now that he's writing up his thesis, but he doesn't have a car and relies on Ben for a ride to get over the mountain."

Billie inhaled to talk more about her boys when Neil looked up. "I have a boy too. His name is Ethan."

Billie exhaled. "Really?" She'd had no idea. "How old is he? What does he do?"

"Early twenties, and he's following in the old footsteps." Neil smiled. "Like your Louis, Ethan's still busy with his education. He's spending hours on the bridge, learning how to chart a course and navigate weather and water."

"So he wants to be a captain like you, your dad, and your grandfather?" Billie liked the idea.

"Yep." Neil pushed the sugar bowl to the side so the server could put the cappuccinos and the pastries on the table. "Thanks." He waited until the server left again and leaned back. "Ethan plans to buy back his grandpa's ferry. It used to belong to our family, you know."

Billie tried her lemon meringue tart. The delightful burst of tangy citrus flavor combined with the airy sweetness of the meringue was delicious. "That'd be great." She liked the idea that Ethan would run the ferry even more than her tart. "The current owner isn't from Mendocino. Don't get me wrong, they're doing a great job. But it'd be nice to have the ferry back in the community, so to speak. We used to be able to call the captain and ask for extra rides if we needed them. The flexibility came in handy. I know two people who were only born in the hospital because your grandpa made emergency runs for their moms."

"I agree. Well, I hope Ethan works it out. What about your boys? Any chance they'll move back home?"

Slowly, Billie nodded. "I think Ben would like to come back. Plus, we do need a vet. It's just a question of money and time. Starting your own praxis isn't cheap. Especially with the property prices up the way they are."

"And Louis?"

"There aren't so many jobs for marine biologists. Louis will have to apply for positions wherever they come up. Honestly, I'm crossing my fingers he'll stay on this continent."

"If he doesn't, I can tell you all the best ways to travel," Neil said, and for a few minutes, they talked about ships and planes and trains while they drank their cappuccinos and ate their pastries. Then Neil checked his watch. "If we want to catch the ferry, we should probably leave."

Billie could have sat longer—much longer. They had barely scraped the surface, and suddenly there were so many more things she wanted to talk about.

"Sure," she said, forcing herself to get up. If Neil got on the ferry with her, he would miss the rest of his party. "It's late already. You should get back to the lighthouse."

He pushed her chair to the table and offered her his arm. "The nice thing about a lighthouse," he mentioned as she slipped her hand on his arm, "is that it won't go anywhere. It'll still be there no matter when I get back."

Billie smiled, and then they walked to the dock where the ferry—decked out in string lights—was already waiting. They were the only people on the upstairs deck, where they watched the bow cut through the glistening water as they talked about the cove, and the island, and what it meant to feel at home.

When they got off the ferry, Neil held Billie's hand to help her over the forever wobbly gangway and opened the door of his waiting car for her.

They drove in silence through the night, apart from when Billie told Neil where to turn.

"This one?" He peered through the window.

"Yes, the little house right here."

"All right." Neil parked in front of her cottage and switched off the engine. "Good night, Billie."

For a moment, Billie considered giving him a goodnight kiss on the cheek. But it was too much. Only twenty-four hours ago, she'd been convinced she couldn't stand the man. So she simply smiled and thanked him for bringing her home, and then she got out of the car and into the cottage, where she pulled the door closed behind her, leaning her back against it until she heard Neil drive off.

When all was safe, Billie pushed away from the door, only now noticing that she still wore his warm jacket over her shoulders. She took it off and for a moment smelled Neil—sun-dried driftwood, salty ocean mist, polished brass, and the smooth cedarwood in the light-house—as if she was still dancing in his arms.

Billie hung the jacket on the hook by the door, letting the length of the sleeve glide through her fingers.

The regret came when she reached the end, and there was nothing to do but to let go.

Why in the world *hadn't* she kissed him goodnight?

CHAPTER 18

Jenny lifted her coffee cup and drank as she watched her daughter and aunt talk across the beautifully set patio table.

Something had changed in the way her two relatives interacted with each other. Something was new. Better.

When she figured it out, Jenny set down her cup. Smiling, she closed her eyes and held her face into the warm morning sun.

They didn't need Jenny anymore to be comfortable with each other. For the first time, Audrey seemed genuinely fond of her great-aunt. She laughed at Aunt Georgie's stories of light-hearted complications on her many cruises. In the latest of the stories, the travel agency had accidentally double-booked Aunt Georgie's suite. When she walked out of her bathroom wrapped in nothing but towels, a man in socks was lying on her bed, leafing through a brochure and screaming in shock when she appeared like a ghost at the foot of the bed.

Both equally smart and eager to leave port, Aunt Georgie and the man in question, Fred, quickly uncovered the cause of their dilemma. Instead of fighting over who should disembark or involving the crew, and with only hours to spare before the ship left port, they cooked up a scheme of pretending they were married and always meant to share the room. What started as a pact of convenience to stay on board soon turned to respect for the other's generosity, smarts, and, Jenny suspected, willingness to share the only available bed. It didn't take long for them to thoroughly fall in love and marry for real.

"Mom? What's your plan for today?" Audrey asked when her great-aunt finished her story.

"I have to be at the university in an hour." Jenny checked her phone for the time. "I would like to submit my research article for publication today. The process always takes longer than I expect."

"Oh, fun. When will it come out?" Georgie asked.

Jenny smiled. "That's up to the reviewers and the editors of the journal. Soon, I hope, but the wheels of academia spin in their own time."

"Good luck, Mom." Audrey poured herself a cup of hot chocolate, artfully spooned whipped cream on it, then finished her creation with a single mint leaf. "The university is going to advertise the professorship position soon, isn't it?"

Jenny nodded. "I got a heads-up from the department chair to be ready to apply. It would be good to at least have one paper submitted when the search committee starts considering the applications."

"You're going to be a *professor*." Aunt Georgie sighed as if she were a mother hen and Jenny spreading her wings for the first time. "Are you sure it's not too much work being a professor? Lazy students and all that?"

Audrey snorted into her cocoa, and Jenny tucked her chin. "We need the money to live, dear aunt," she said reasonably. "Food and all that."

"Oh, you do need money. That's right." Aunt Georgie sounded as if she only now remembered that not all her family was wealthy.

"Yes." Jenny smiled and crossed her arms over her chest. "Aunt Georgie, we need to talk about the hotel."

"What about it?" Aunt Georgie's eyes slid to the side as she took a sip of coffee.

Jenny took a deep breath. She'd given her aunt space to come to terms with her memories and adjust her worldview a little. "Audrey would like to reopen the hotel. As you know, she's a hotel manager. A very capable one at that."

"Yes, she is. I could tell the moment I saw my swan towel in the bathroom that first night." Aunt Georgie set her cup down. "You are," she assured Audrey, who beamed back.

"So what do you think, Auntie?" Audrey asked breathlessly. "About reopening the hotel?"

"I think the hotel is cursed, child," Aunt Georgie said slowly. "I think you should get out and away as soon as you can." She turned to Jenny. "You too, darling. You have become way too comfortable here. I wish I'd never allowed you to come back. I thought the hotel would be more run-down than it is. You weren't supposed to make it so...nice."

Audrey stood. The joy in her blue eyes had turned dark in disbelief. She held out a hand, gesturing toward the beach. "But, Auntie! How can this be cursed? Look at how beautiful it is!"

Aunt Georgie didn't look. "I already know how beautiful it is," she murmured. "That doesn't mean it isn't cursed. I don't want anything to happen to you."

"Aunt Georgie." Jenny motioned for Audrey to sit back down. "It's not cursed. My mother lost her way."

"How could she lose her way?" Aunt Georgie shook her head. "She knew the way as well as I did. I should never have left her alone, but how could she lose her way so thoroughly in half an hour? It doesn't make a lick of sense. Not back then, not now, and not in all the years in between."

Audrey sat back down, eyes wide.

"I don't know." Jenny shook her head. "Maybe a snake did bite her, and she was incapacitated. It is possible she lost consciousness." Jenny had researched snake bites long before Neil had even found his father's journal. While a snake bite was unlikely, it was not impossible. If enough time passed, the venom didn't even show up on a tox screen—at least not back then. Jenny had looked that up, too.

"Didn't you say Neil's dad thought it was a snake bite?" Audrey asked as if she could read her mother's mind. "I was going to ask, but I didn't meet him at the party last night."

"Ray passed away years ago, Audrey. He just wrote in his journal that he thought it likely was a snake bite."

Jenny was still watching her aunt. She'd accidentally dropped that juicy bit of information, but Aunt Georgie hadn't heard her say it yet.

But her daughter wasn't so easily satisfied. "Wait, Mom. Why did he write about Grandma Willow in his journal? Was he in love with her?"

"There was a journal?" Aunt Georgie asked.

Jenny turned to look at Audrey. She had not meant to open this can of worms. "Neil's dad was the firefighter who found your grandmother," she said quietly. "Naturally, he wondered what happened. We all did."

"Maybe he *was* in love with her," Aunt Georgie said. "Jenny? Did you read his journal?"

Jenny blinked. "There was no reason. Neil said his dad was distraught over losing someone local, someone so close to...his own age..." She allowed her words to trail away.

For a while, they sat in silence. "Maybe I should ask to see the journal," Jenny said then.

"Maybe you should." Aunt Georgie put a half-eaten croissant back down on her plate.

Jenny folded her napkin, set it carefully beside her plate, and stood. "Audrey? Would you mind clearing the table while I make a call?"

"Sure, Mom." Audrey glanced at her great-aunt. "Auntie? You still have a full plate. I could show you a sketch of the kitchen renovation I was thinking about while you finish your breakfast."

This seemed to rattle Aunt Georgie from her thoughts. "The kitchen is perfectly fine the way it is!"

she said indignantly. "What on earth do you want to renovate it for, child?"

Audrey started arguing her case while pouring hot coffee and sweet cream for her great-aunt.

Jenny smiled as she walked inside to call Neil. Audrey was good for Aunt Georgie—and vice versa. The two should run the hotel together.

"Neil?"

"Jenny. How are you?"

"Great. It was a lovely party last night. Thank you for inviting us over."

"Thank you for coming. I'm happy to say that we raised enough to repair the beacon. This time next week, the old lighthouse might shine again."

"That's wonderful, Neil. Hey, listen."

"What's up?"

Jenny came right to the point. "I was wondering whether you read more of your dad's journal."

"I haven't had time. You would like to see it, would you?"

She smiled. "I would. Specifically, I wonder whether...um..." It felt silly to say it out loud.

"What? It's all right. You can tell me."

"We always knew Willow was hiding a secret." Jenny hadn't meant to say the words. Almost, they surprised her.

It took Neil a moment to reply. "You think Ray knew her secret?"

Jenny exhaled. "I really have no idea. It just seems like he thought about her a lot. More, maybe, than can be explained by just him finding her."

"Do you think?"

"He was a firefighter, after all. I bet he wasn't easily rattled." Willow wasn't the first victim found by firefighters—between the wild forest and the rugged coast, the locals and the tourists...accidents happened every few years.

"That's true, he wasn't easily rattled. Your mom wasn't his first...local accident." Neil cleared his throat. "I thought it was because they were close in age. It was easy for him to identify with her. A little too close for comfort, if you know what I mean."

"Well, I was wondering whether we might have another look at his journal. I realize it's private. But if you don't mind... We still have so many questions without answers."

"It's no problem at all, Jenny. We'll have a second look and see what Dad has to say for himself." He sounded as if he was smiling.

"Thank you. I'll come over," Jenny offered. "I have to go to Lizzie May to teach a class first, but I could come right after. I can help clean up the rest of the party too."

"All taken care of—I got up early to clean so I could have a quiet evening. Come over when you're done with work. I'll be here."

"Thank you, Neil." Jenny checked her watch. "I'll be there around five if that works. I'll try not to take up too much of your time. A quick scan should be enough to tell us more."

Jenny hung up just as Audrey and Aunt Georgie passed through the living room on their way to the kitchen.

"And?" Eyebrows raised, Audrey stopped. "Is he going to let you read the journal?"

"We'll read it together. I'll know more tonight." Jenny grabbed her bag, which was waiting on the sofa, and kissed first her daughter, then her aunt, on the cheek. "Now I have to run. Bye, my two darlings. Don't do anything I wouldn't do. In particular, redo the kitchen and or sell the hotel."

Chapter 19

J enny raised her voice. "For your homework, I want you to delve deeper into the whaling history of Nantucket. Choose one aspect we covered already that resonates with you—it could be the role of women in whaling communities, the impact of technology on the industry, or even the cultural significance of tales and stories revolving around whaling. Research and then write a brief essay or create a presentation about your chosen topic, highlighting its importance and relevance to our understanding of Nantucket's past. Be prepared to share your findings and insights in our next class!"

The groan of protest rising from her students was lost in the general chatting, laughing, and shuffling of feet and backpacks as Jenny's students gathered their things and made for the exit of the lecture hall.

"Don't cheat!" she called into the noise, smiling. "I know all y'alls work partners and will check!"

Someone grinned and waved, and Jenny waved back.

"Going well so far?" The chair of the history department, Carolina Perez, had fought her way through the tide of students and appeared beside Jenny at the lectern.

"I think so." Jenny waited until the last student left the lecture hall. "It was a choppy start, but we've found our way." She chuckled, thinking about the first lecture she'd given. She'd had to take the students outside and sit them on the bluff like kindergartners before they would pay attention.

"You're doing great. I hear things."

"You hear things?"

"Some of your students are in my class. They talk when they think I'm not paying attention. But I'm always paying attention." Carolina adjusted her reading glasses and scrolled through her phone.

"Are those new?" Jenny loaded her arms with her laptop, books, and the messy piles of homework papers the students had left on the lectern.

"They are. I just got them, and I *hate* them. Also lose them every two minutes. Here." Carolina had found what she was looking for. "The search committee just posted our job advertisement. I want you to apply right away. I'm sending it to your email."

"Thanks." Jenny's stomach sunk a notch. "I really want this job. I hope I have enough to make my case."

"You've got teaching experience in the classes we're looking for. That's not nothing." Carolina looked over the brim of the half-glasses. "Did you submit the paper last night?"

"Just this morning," Jenny admitted. "I wanted another glance before sending it off."

"Did you already get a confirmation from the editor?"

Jenny pulled out her own phone and tapped on the email app, trying to balance the loose-leaf pile of homework. "Yes. There it is." She held up her proof.

"Good." Carolina tucked away her own phone again. "It's not much, but it's a start. Good luck with the application, Jenny. I hope the committee will pick you."

"Thank you." Jenny had hoped Carolina would be on the committee. Jenny's meager CV could have used a staunch supporter. "Fingers crossed."

Carolina nodded, turned on her heel, and marched out.

Jenny took a deep breath. She needed the job. Aunt Georgie was still saying she wanted to sell the hotel. At least they now knew what made her want to forget—or sell—the hotel. A superstitious belief that the hotel was a bad place for Jenny and Audrey.

Maybe she believed her sister had met with foul play.

Maybe she even believed the perpetrator was still out there, ready to harm the tiny rest of her family.

Clutching her papers, Jenny hurried out of the room.

She was already late meeting Neil, and he'd sounded like he had hoped for a quiet, visitor-free evening. Besides, Jon had called earlier, asking her to spend the evening at the winery with him. And that was exactly what Jenny wanted too.

In her office, she picked up her bag and folders. Walking toward the parking lot with her precariously teetering cargo, she texted Jon with one thumb.

Might be late.

It was all she managed before a file folder slipped
and fell to the ground, and she had to stop and
rearrange everything so she could pick up the folder.
Feeling frazzled and too hot, she finally reached her
car and tossed everything in the trunk.

As she was walking to the driver's seat, Jenny's
phone beeped.

Can we grab coffee this afternoon? Billie asked.

Wiping a few beads of sweat from her forehead,
Jenny texted back. *Busy today... Tomorrow?*

Jenny opened her door, threw herself into the seat,
pressed the buttons for the AC, and started the car.

Jon didn't text back, and she considered calling
him as she drove the winding road along the coast
toward the Mendocino Cove harbor. But then she
remembered he was working out in the vineyard today. He was probably gloved up, holding twine with
his teeth, sweat running into his eyes, and hands full
of tools. It would be a bother for him to answer a call.

Since she didn't have much to say anyway, Jenny
decided to call him later and spent the rest of her
drive putting together her CV for the application in
her mind.

Miraculously, she caught a car spot on the ferry.
Soon after, she pulled up in front of the old lighthouse, parked, and got out.

The afternoon sun was still high in the sky, which
had been a foggy sapphire blue all day. But now, white,
dense streaks of clouds drifted in from the northwest.
A sudden chill in the sea breeze made Jenny rub her

arms as she knocked on the door of the lighthouse and stepped back.

The door opened, and there stood Neil. Clearly taking his day off, he had replaced his swanky suit from the evening before with gray sweatpants and a cozy long-sleeved Henley shirt. His hair looked like he'd just woken up and rolled out of bed, and his jaw sported a five o'clock shadow.

"Hey." Jenny smiled.

"Hey." He blinked sleepily and waited for her to come inside. "Good seeing you."

She laughed. "Yeah, right. I woke you up."

He grinned and scratched his chin. "It got late last night. I had too much coffee and decided to dismantle the dance floor before going to bed. I might've taken a little nap just now."

Jenny looked around the wild garden before he closed the door. "Did they already pick up the tables and chairs?"

He yawned and nodded. "Yep. It's all cleaned up and back to normal again. Tea?"

"Sure. Neil, I'm so sorry I dropped by without giving you too much of a heads-up. I really appreciate you doing this for me. I'll get out of your hair as soon as possible."

Clearly unbothered, he waved the apology away. "No worries. It's fine."

Jenny wanted to ask about the coffee—there hadn't been any at the buffet last night. But he had brought Billie home and stayed away longer than any of them had expected. Maybe that was why Billie had wanted to talk?

Jenny climbed the stairs, feeling bad about putting her friend off until the next day. Billie had been there for her every step of the way when Jenny had needed a friend herself. Silently, she promised herself to call Billie as soon as she left the lighthouse. Jon, too.

"Here." Neil pushed open the door to the cozy living room with the fireplace and let Jenny enter. "Have a seat."

"Okay. Thanks." Rubbing her arms, Jenny sat in one of the armchairs.

"I just made hot peppermint tea. Give me a second." Neil brought a pot of tea from the kitchen and pulled the journal out of the bookshelf. "How about a fire?" he asked when he came back to her. "You're still cold."

She turned to look at him. "Just a little," she admitted. "But you don't need to make a fire, Neil. We have tea, and I was even too hot earlier, wishing it would cool down. I'll be fine."

"You'll get your wish, then. The hot weather is breaking." He glanced out of the window. "It's going to break in a grand way."

A chill ran down Jenny's spine. She tried not to shiver, but her shoulders twitched involuntarily.

He smiled. "Well, I'll make a fire for myself, then. I feel like having one."

"Oh." She smiled back, a little embarrassed at being caught out. "Well, far be it from me to argue. And to be perfectly honest, I would *love* a fire. I was just being coy."

"I know. Stop thinking you're bothering me. I like having you here." Neil winked at Jenny. "Here, hold on to it while I build the fire." He handed her the journal. "Don't want to drop that in the grate with the kindling."

Jenny took the journal from his hands, and Neil started stacking cedar kindling and birch logs into the fireplace. Soon, the cedar's pleasant resinous scent mixed with that of the fragrant peppermint tea and the lovely aroma of old books.

The journal burned under Jenny's fingertips. "Do you mind if I have a look?"

"Jenny—I'd rather be the one reading it to you." Neil blew into the heart of the flames, fanning them to burn brighter. "My dad was no saint. I feel like I'd better throw myself in between Ray's deepest, darkest thoughts and your innocent blue angel eyes."

Jenny chuckled at the thought of having innocent angel eyes—or anyone needing to protect them. But Neil had a point. "You're right. I don't know your dad, and I wouldn't like a stranger to read my journal either."

"Something like that." Flames crackled and cheerfully licked up the dry logs. Neil brushed the wood dust off his hands and sat in the other armchair.

Jenny handed him the notebook, and he flipped it open. "What exactly are we looking for?"

Jenny cleared her throat. "Reasons why he would go so far as requesting the toxicology report for my mother," she said. "Reasons he was out there searching for her when the official search had been called off. Reasons...reasons for searching for her in the right spot. Reasons, I suppose, why he was the one who found her."

Neil frowned. "You don't think he had anything to do with your mom's death, do you? Dad wasn't a saint. But he was a good man. One of the best, in my eyes."

"Of course he was. I never doubted that for a second. I still remember his face when he talked to Grandma. I knew even back then he was a good man with a kind heart." Jenny sat up straighter. "I mean...other sorts of reasons."

Neil's frown deepened. "Like?"

"Oh, Neil." Jenny exhaled and sank back into her chair. "The question is, was Ray in love with Willow?"

CHAPTER 20

B illie pulled the brush one more time through her short curls. Critically, she turned in front of the bedroom mirror.

She'd changed out of her jeans and hoodie into the new dress. The dress looked nice enough. But she herself—she was no big prize. Her legs were too short; her belly showed. And while her hair was still dark, the crinkly lines around her eyes gave away her age.

With a sigh, she turned away.

She would just go, knock on the door, hand over the jacket, and get herself back home. If Neil asked why she'd gone to all the trouble when she could've just kept the jacket until their next accidental meeting, she would tell him that she'd gone shopping on the island, and it was convenient to return it. Could be he needed it.

Or something.

It wasn't the best plan. But Billie hadn't slept too well, and she was never at her brainiest when she was tired.

Maybe it was only her imagination. But last night, it sure had seemed as if Neil had enjoyed her company as much as she'd enjoyed his.

Now, in the light of a new, sober day, she wasn't so sure anymore. It was possible that Lex or Jon had asked Neil to bring her home. And then...

"You're just *desperate*," she murmured to herself. "You also thought *Ian* wanted to get back together. I mean, come *on*, Billie. How pathetic are we today?"

"What was that?" Her brother knocked on the open door, already entering.

Startled, Billie put a hand to her heart. "Jon! What are you doing here? You scared me."

He laughed and held up his hands in peace. "I called out for you! I really thought you had fainted or something. Your truck is out front, so I knew you were home."

Billie dropped her hand back down. "Well, come in, I guess."

Her brother sat on the edge of her bed. "You look very pretty." He nodded at her dress. "What's happening? Are you going out?"

"No," Billie said defensively, but then she sighed and sat next to her brother. "Full disclosure? I was going to return the jacket Neil loaned me last night."

He smiled. "Aha."

"Is the dress too much?" She tugged on the skirt. "Tell me the truth."

Jon patted her arm. "The dress is lovely. Unlike me, Neil doesn't know yet that you usually run around in jeans and T-shirts, so he won't think anything of it. I mean...won't think anything other than that you're beautiful."

Billie grimaced. "It's too much. I'll go change."

"No. No." Jon chuckled. "I'm being serious. Don't change. He'll appreciate it."

"For real?"

Jon put an arm around her shoulders and drew her to him. "Why so insecure all of a sudden? That's not like you at all. What happened?"

"I like him." Billie put a hand in front of her mouth and stared at her brother.

"You do?" The smile spread to Jon's eyes.

"I do. I didn't mean to. But I really enjoyed talking with him yesterday."

"I told you he was a great guy." Jon let her go again. "I suppose it doesn't hurt that he's in great shape and belongs to one of the oldest families on the island?"

"That...doesn't matter." Billie threw Jon a stern glance but couldn't keep it up. "Well, those things *are* nice. But I knew about them before he and I had coffee together last night. It was talking with him that changed my mind."

"Is that why he was gone forever? You two had coffee?"

She nodded. "Near the ferry dock. There's a new café."

"I heard about it. Well." Jon let himself fall backward on the bed, interlocking his fingers behind his head. "It's not like everyone didn't know you two were perfect for each other."

"You *don't* know that," Billie said. But secretly, she was pleased. "Maybe *he* doesn't like *me*."

"Then he wouldn't leave his own party to hang out with you. Grow up, Bills. He's head over heels, poor man."

"Nah...why on earth would he?" Billie's cheeks flushed warmly, and she turned away to hide her cheeks.

What if Neil *was* head over heels? What if he wanted more than she was ready—or rather, comfortable—to give?

After her divorce, Billie had been fed up with the entire institution of men and love and romance, so she swore off the whole shebang. She hadn't dated a man in too many years to count. What if they would kiss? It wasn't that she was strictly opposed to it. But *how* to kiss? She honestly couldn't remember.

"Billie." Jon reached out and took her hand. "Baby sister. He's a good man. You two *are* perfect for each other. I wasn't teasing when I said that."

"No?"

"All these years, you worried about me and my relationships." Jon smiled. "At least I had some. You had none. I won't say I worried, but I wished you would find someone. I hoped. You're not the solitary kind, and we all need someone to hold us. Someone beside whom we can wake up and who greets us with a smile. Someone to catch us when we fall. We all deserve that. I do. You certainly do. And, my dear, Neil does too. Don't you think?"

Billie looked at their hands. "I'm so glad you are my brother," she said quietly. "Thanks, Jon."

Jon pressed a kiss on her hand and let go. "So go and return the jacket and wear a pretty dress for your lighthouse keeper. I'm almost one hundred percent certain Neil's at home, working up the nerve to call you."

She smiled. "Last night, I felt like he might call today. Only he hasn't. What does that do to your percentage of certainty?"

"Still at ninety-nine," Jon said and pulled himself into a sitting position. "He's probably recovering from being social last night. Be a modern woman and ask him out before he does."

"Should I?" Billie stood and went back to the mirror, pulling the dress in place.

"Do you *want* to?"

She turned. "Yes. I do. In fact..."

"What?"

She grimaced. "TMI, but I was sorry I didn't kiss him goodnight last night."

Jon laughed. "Not as sorry as he was, I bet." He stood as well. "I was going to see him today too, matter of fact. I still have some tools of his, and I know he needs them back for the beacon room."

"And me with the jacket?" Billie chuckled. "We can't show up one after the other, each returning something. That's silly."

"Let's go together, then. When you give me the secret sign, I'll evaporate so you can finally give him last night's kiss."

"If I still feel like it. And if he even wants it." Billie's doubts bubbled up again as she looked at her middle-aged reflection.

"I don't hate much, but I hate what that louse Ian did to your self-esteem." Jon stepped beside Billie, lowering his face next to hers in the mirror. "You used to be so confident when it came to your heart."

It was true. Before she met Ian, she'd been different. But that was a long time ago. "Yeah, well, I was young and naive, and my confidence didn't serve me too well." Billie swallowed.

"But you're not twenty anymore. You're wiser now and more experienced, and, may I say it, kinder and sweeter. Pair that with the confidence that always belonged to you, and you'll be invincible. I want you to claim yourself again, Billie," Jon murmured. "It's time."

Slowly, Billie nodded.

Jon was right. Of course Neil liked her. Out of all the people at the party taking the ferry back home the night before, Neil insisted on accompanying her.

"You're right," she whispered, leaning her head against her brother's. "It's time."

"Come on." Jon smiled at their reflection. "Let's go pay Neil a surprise visit."

CHAPTER 21

Sitting cross-legged in front of the glowing fireplace, Neil stopped flipping through the journal and laid it open on the floor. "Here. This is the page where Dad first mentions Willow."

Jenny got out of her armchair and sat beside him on the hearthrug. Her head was swimming now that the room was getting warmer, and a feeling of unreality had settled over her. She blinked, but the words were shifting position. She rubbed her eyes with the palm of her hand. "You read it to me, Neil."

"Are you okay?" He looked at her.

"Yes." She closed her eyes. "Read. Please."

"Jenny, lean on me—you look pale."

"Okay." Jenny scooted closer and leaned against the lighthouse keeper, resting her head on his shoulder while the glow from the fire reflected warmly off her face.

"Dad wrote this one in 1992," Neil said softly.

"The year Mom went missing," Jenny whispered.

"Yes. But he wrote it earlier in the year, before it happened." Neil cleared his throat and read out loud.

The moment I saw her again after all these years, my heart raced like it never skipped a beat. Willow's laughter echoed in my ears, reminding me of the days before I left, when we were inseparable. Our past may have ended with a fight, but this newfound connection between us feels like a second chance at happiness.

"Our past may have ended with a fight... They knew each other before he left." Jenny nodded, her eyes still closed, her cheek moving against the soft Henley fabric of Neil's shirt as she spoke the words. "They were lovers before he left the island. Of course they were."

"A second chance at happiness," Neil repeated slowly. "It does sound like it, doesn't it? Wow." He paused before he continued. "The next entry is a couple days later." He read.

Last night, we walked along the shore, hand in hand. The moonlight danced on her hair, and I felt a warmth I'd almost forgotten. I've loved her since the moment I met her, even when years and miles kept us apart. I still don't know why she was suddenly so angry with me back then, but our last fight was the push I needed to fulfill my dream of traveling the world. Sometimes, I wonder if that's exactly what she wanted, if all along, she only had my happiness in mind. My love for her feels deeper and more profound than anything I ever felt before. I am sure now, that in this world, I am meant to be with Willow. I want to make this work, to be a part of her life once more.

"Neil." Jenny wanted to straighten her back, but she was too stunned. "They got together again after you and your dad returned to the island. They were secretly dating. They were lovers."

"I had no idea. None."

Now, Jenny opened her eyes. "Neil, I never asked... Who is your mother?"

"Her name was Adriana. She lived in San Francisco but passed away a few years ago."

"I'm so sorry."

"Yeah." Neil ran a hand through his hair. "She and Dad got divorced shortly after I was born. She moved to Monterey and left Dad to raise me on the island. Once Dad started to take bigger ships on longer trips, I sometimes did stay with her while he was gone."

"That sounds... Was that okay for you?"

"You mean moving back and forth?" He nodded. "For me, it worked out just fine. My parents married for all the wrong reasons and became much better friends after they divorced. Splitting was the best decision they ever made." He chuckled.

"I'm sure they both loved you very much."

"Yes, they did." Neil put an arm around Jenny's shoulders and pulled her closer. "But you know how you have a certain image of your past in your head? If Dad loved Willow... I think my image just flipped upside down. All that time I thought it was just him and me." He shook his head.

Jenny smiled. Her image had never solidified. She'd always lived with the blanks in her history. Maybe it was even the reason she'd become a historian. "Let's remind ourselves it's the past. Whatever we know or don't know—it already happened the way it happened. Finding out about it doesn't change anything."

Slowly, he nodded. "So our parents were lovers," he murmured. "Willow and Ray."

For a while, they watched the flames, thinking.

"You know," Jenny said softly, "Mom never told me who my father is."

A long breath escaped Neil. "You don't know?"

Jenny shook her head. "She never said."

The muscles in Neil's jaw tensed. "Let's do the math, shall we?"

"I just did. The timing works out. It is possible I'm Ray's daughter."

His hand tightened on her shoulder. "Really?"

Together, they went through the numbers again. "He left Mendocino Island before you were born," Neil murmured. "Even before Willow's pregnancy would have shown. I swear that if Ray was your father, he did not know."

"I agree." Jenny looked at him. "Mom was fiercely independent. She knew Ray had just been released from an unhappy marriage and wanted to travel the world. Not in a million years would she have held him back. I can absolutely imagine Mom picking a fight to alienate Ray so he would leave before she showed and things got complicated."

Neil exhaled a tense breath. "He'd have stayed for you, Jenny. I know him."

Jenny moistened her lips. "And that's exactly what Mom didn't want. She wanted everyone to go after their dreams with every last shred and fiber of their soul. *Especially* those she loved. She did the same for herself. It was the only way she could live."

Jenny shifted her weight and stretched her legs, just for a moment of moving, of changing her body as her mind adjusted to a new reality.

The secret in her mother's past was part of Jenny's DNA. Deep in her genes resided a love Willow couldn't share and Jenny couldn't picture.

Suddenly having a name and a face—a whole person—who could well be her father was a shock. As if the gap in her genes snapped shut with a boom that only reverberated in her own ears.

She shook her head to make the ringing of the boom's echo go away. This was a time to focus.

"Let's see what else Dad has to say for himself." Neil flipped over the page in the journal and scanned the words. "A couple of entries about the lighthouse... I'll read those later. Here, listen to this one." Again, he cleared his throat to read.

Walking across the bluff, I caught a glimpse of her and her daughter collecting mussels on the beach below. It was a fleeting moment, but I saw the expression in Willow's eyes when she spotted me. I know she recognized me. I know she was telling me something. Is it possible? Could this beautiful teenager be ours? The math, the timing, and most of all the look in Willow's eyes—it all points to the possibility. My heart races at the thought of having a daughter.

"Oh." Jenny pressed her fingers to her lips to stifle the sob rising in her throat.

Neil glanced at her, then turned to the next page.

Today, Willow and I finally started to talk about the past, carefully unearthing old memories and feelings. My heart aches with the longing I've held on to for so long. I wanted to tell her everything at once, confess my love and regret, but the words got stuck in my throat. A single mother, at that time, in this small town? I should have been there for her. I didn't know. I didn't know. I didn't know. And yet, excuses do nothing to calm my guilt and anger at myself. I should have known.

"He didn't tell her that he loved her?"

"Not everything, it seems. Let's read on." The muscles in Neil's shoulder tensed, and Jenny put a hand on his forearm. He took a breath. "It's...something else, isn't it?"

"He didn't know," Jenny said softly. "I don't think he gives my mom enough credit for her part in this. Willow didn't want him to know."

"The date is getting closer to when your Mom went missing. Are you sure you want to keep reading?"

Jenny nodded. After all these many years of speculating and worrying and wondering, knowing was better than not knowing.

Neil bowed his head back over the journal and took a breath to read.

I look at Willow and see a future together, a chance to finally be the family we should have been. I'll make sure she knows how much she means to me, every single day. I asked her to meet me in the forest, in the fern grove where we used to spend our afternoons. I think I sized the ring correctly. It should fit. It has to fit. It has to be perfect.

"Oh, no." Jenny put her face into her hands as puzzle pieces started to slide in her head, bumping into empty places that looked like they would fit. "Please, no."

"Do you want me to stop?" Neil's voice was hoarse.

She didn't look up but shook her head. He continued, his voice gentle.

My world shattered. I told the chief we'd arranged to meet in the fern grove. A day later, she still hasn't returned, and we haven't found her. Her mother and sister were at the trailhead today, frantic with fear. The chief ordered me to go home and grab an hour of sleep before heading out again, but he can't force me. I can hear the new search teams out there, combing the forest and calling her name.

Neil looked up. "There are smudges on the page. He wrote this in the forest. How are you holding up?"

"I feel sick to the stomach."

"You look pale. More tomorrow? Maybe we should go take a walk, get some color back in your cheeks?"

Jenny shook her head. Now, she needed to know the rest. "Read the next one."

"It's short." His eyebrows rose as he scanned ahead.

Someone found the dog's collar near the trail. It looks like it had been cut so he'd rip loose.

"Bobby's collar was *cut*?" Jenny looked up. "That explains *that*. It was brand-new. Georgie had only just bought it, and she couldn't understand how it would rip."

"Hmm." A line appeared between Neil's eyes. He stood to put more wood on the fire and push together the glowing embers, then sat back beside her again. "Okay?"

She nodded.

Today, the detectives talked to me. I was still in the firehouse with the guys when she disappeared from the trail, so they let me go again. Her mother looked as if she didn't believe me and said Willow could find the fern grove wearing a blindfold at night. I know this is true; she knew the way by heart. If she were anywhere near the grove, we would have found her. Fear eats at my heart. Where is she? What have I done?

"Mom was trying to meet Ray that day," Jenny whispered. "She needed Aunt Georgie to drive her to the trailhead because her car was in the shop. Was she trying to make Aunt Georgie go back to the car on purpose so she could meet Ray in secret?" Had Willow herself cut the collar of Aunt Georgie's dog so she could get rid of her sister? Jenny's thoughts swirled in a dizzying hurricane. There had been an argument between the sisters in the car. About the dog. Willow had gripped Bobby too tightly, and Georgie had been upset.

"Should 1 stop here? There are a couple more entries." Neil stood to poke the wood in the grate. It toppled, and a spark flew on the hearthrug. Neil stepped on it, but he had a faraway look in his eyes.

"Let's read it all." Jenny hugged her knees.

He sat back down beside her, tucking her under his arm. "Remember that it already happened," he murmured. "It's already over. Reading this doesn't change the past."

She nodded. "Go on."

"This one's a few days later."

Still no sign of Willow. An accident. A cougar, or a rattle snake. Can't sleep, can't eat. Every moment without her feels like an eternity. I can't help but replay our last moments together in my mind. Luckily, Neil spends all his time with his friends.

"I did. I was glad to finally be home again. But how could he hide all this from me? Talk about teens being oblivious." Shaking his head, Neil flipped the page.

The official searches have ended, but I can't give up on her. We've scoured the grove and the forest, followed every lead, every broken twig and fallen leaf, but there's nothing. My soul aches with every step, and I'm consumed by a mix of desperation and dread. Her mother won't talk to me. She talks to nobody.

"Poor man," Jenny whispered.

Neil growled low in his throat, agreeing with her. For a moment, he stared at the next page before reading it out loud.

Two weeks since she disappeared, and today, I found her. Willow's lifeless body among the towering redwoods, hidden by a fallen root. It's a nightmare I can't wake up from. My heart screams in agony, and I'm left with unanswerable questions. Why her? Why now?

"Yeah." Jenny sighed at the inevitable conclusion of the story.

"That's just horrible." Frowning, Neil returned to the spot he marked with a finger. "Last entry, Jenny."

"Read it," she whispered.

He murmured, "Not sure *I* can take more of this," but did as she'd asked.

I can't find words to describe the pain. The woman I loved, who was finally back in my life, is gone forever. I struggle to—

Neil stopped and let the journal sink.

"That's it?" Jenny looked up.

"That's it." Neil flipped through the last pages, but there were no more entries. "Soon after that, Dad left the island to take a job on a container ship. I barely saw him before I went to the academy. Now I know why."

"Neil?"

"Yeah?" He looked at her.

"I think we're siblings. Brother and sister."

For a moment, Jenny couldn't tell whether tears were swimming in her eyes or her brother's. She blinked.

"Come here." Neil turned and pulled Jenny into his arms, hugging her to him. "My little sister," he whispered.

Jenny was about to reply when the door behind them burst open.

CHAPTER 22

Neil tensed, but Jenny didn't care. She couldn't look up to see who had come in. Overcome by what she'd learned, she stayed where she was, her face tucked into Neil's shoulder.

"Jenny?" Jon's voice was sharp, a tone she'd never heard before. "Neil! What's going on? Is she okay?"

Jenny lifted her tear-stained face. "I'm okay, Jon. I'm..."

In a moment, Jon kneeled beside her. "Neil, what's going on?"

Without missing a beat, she slung her arms around Jon's neck. Jon was her rock; she needed to hold on to him.

"I think... Jenny? Is it all right if I share?" Neil wanted her permission to explain, and she nodded.

The door clicked shut again.

"Go on, Neil." Jon stood, taking Jenny with him. He sat on one of the armchairs, and Jenny cuddled up to him. "What happened here, my brother?"

"We were reading my dad's journal." Neil rose and walked to the fireplace. "Turns out that he and Jenny's mom..." He cleared his throat and tried again. "It turns out that there's a good chance Jenny and I are related. Half-siblings, or whatever it's called."

Jenny felt better now that Jon was here. She lifted her head. "Neil and I are brother and sister, Jon."

Jon's hold tightened around her waist. "For real?"

"For real. I mean...we don't have actual proof." Jenny took a deep breath. "We should do a test, shouldn't we, Neil?" She looked over her shoulder.

Neil smiled at her. However the news might have shaken him, he looked as if he liked the idea of having her for a sister. "Sure. We'll do a test. But I have a feeling it's true."

"I have that feeling too," Jenny said and smiled back. "Right from the beginning, you felt like a big brother to me."

Neil looked over her head. His smile faded.

Jenny turned to see what he was seeing and only now noticed Billie was standing quietly by the door. "Billie!" She stood, glad to see her friend.

"Hey, Jenny." Billie smiled back. But it wasn't her usual wide, generous smile.

"Here. Sit a moment longer." Jon stood to give Jenny the chair, and she sat. She hadn't eaten anything since breakfast, and now it showed.

"Come in, please, Billie. Take a chair." Neil had gone to Billie, offering his hand.

Mechanically, she put her hand into his, and he led her to his armchair. Billie sat.

Jon and Neil stood before them, frowning, until Jenny could think straight again. "What a shock that was," she said then.

Neil turned to Jon. "Erm, how did you even get into the lighthouse?"

Jon raised an eyebrow. "The door was open. We called. Didn't you hear us?"

"I told him we shouldn't go inside and disturb you," Billie murmured. "We were just going to put your suit jacket and the tools Jon borrowed on the table. I'm sorry for barging in, Neil."

"I'm not," Jon said dryly. "Jenny's car is parked outside. Of course the love of my life can do whatever she wants, but I'm no fool either." He turned to Neil. "If it would've come down to you or me, Bennett, you'd have lost that fight."

Neil looked amused. "You'd have battled me for the hand of your woman, Donovan?"

"You bet." Jon put a finger under Jenny's chin, tipping her face up so he could see her eyes. "Just in case that test comes back negative... Don't try anything, brother. She's mine."

"Goodness, Jon, how silly. I don't belong to anyone but myself." Against her will, Jenny had to smile.

"I gotta say, Donovan, I'm surprised it took you as long as it did to find her. Do a better job looking out for my sister, if you possibly can," Neil said. "Or I'll do it."

"I don't need your help. Never needed it, never will."

"Did you bring my tools back, or are you going to fight me for those too?"

Jon grinned. "Downstairs."

Neil glanced at Billie, and when he spoke next, his voice was changed. "I'm sorry about all this, Billie. The doorbell is as old as the lighthouse. Gramps always said he was going to fix it, but it never happened."

"I forgot to return your jacket last night." Billie sounded cautious. Jenny smiled. She'd never seen her friend be shy before.

"I didn't forget." Neil smiled. "I left it on purpose with you. I meant to go back to get it today and use the occasion to ask you out for another coffee."

"You want to take my little sister out on a *date*, Bennett?" Jon asked sternly.

"Jon!" Billie called out, scandalized.

Neil threw him a cold look. "Since you're dating *my* sister, you'd better be all for it, Donovan."

It was so silly Billie and Jenny both started laughing. A knot loosened in the center of Jenny's being. With every new laugh bubbling out of her, more of the dark secrets in her past left. New air filled the old, sad spaces with joy and happiness making it feel like she could never stop laughing. Tears dropped from her eyes and rolled down her cheeks until Billie was hugging her, laughing just because Jenny was.

"Maybe warm tea and toast with cheese will help," Neil said wryly at some point and left. Jon sat down on the arm of Jenny's chair and waited until Jenny could stop.

"Are you feeling better now?" Billie asked and wiped the tears from Jenny's face with a tissue she pulled from the pocket of her nice dress.

Jenny nodded. It really was a *very* nice dress. Billie looked fabulous. "I'm so sorry, you two," she said. "I feel like I've been through the wringer."

"I can't believe you two are really related." Billie sat back down. "Tell me everything."

"It's all in his dad's journal," Jenny said and nodded at the book on the rug before the fire. "Ray and Willow were lovers around the time I was conceived. Ray left without knowing Mom was pregnant. When he returned, he asked my mom to meet him in their old special spot in the forest so he could propose to her. I think Mom might have cut the dog's collar to set up Aunt Georgie because she wanted to slip away and meet Ray."

"But she couldn't get to the old spot."

"And Ray never got over losing her," Jenny said. "He thought her death was his fault for asking her to meet him in the forest."

"It wasn't anyone's fault," Jon said gently. "Not his, not Willow's, not yours, and not Georgie's. It was an accident, whether it was a snake bite or a lost trail."

The door opened again, and Neil appeared with an enormous wooden tray laden with a big, steaming teapot, a sugar bowl and cream, and a tower of cheese sandwiches. "Sweet peppermint tea for the nerves," he said and set the tray on the small table between the armchairs. "Billie? How about it?"

Billie seemed to have recovered her composure. "I don't mind a cup of hot, sweet tea, to be honest," she said. "Thanks, Neil."

"Anytime, my dear." He filled a cup and handed it to Billie. Their fingertips touched when she took it, and their eyes locked.

Jenny looked at Jon, and they smiled at each other. Jon held out a hand, and Jenny took it, rising from her chair. "Actually," she announced brightly, "Neil, I really need fresh air to...well, to air out my brain."

Neil tore his gaze from Billie and turned to her. "I can open a window if you like."

"No, that's all right. Billie looks cold." Jon led Jenny to the door. "Bills, make sure you get warm and cozy. I'll pick you up in twenty minutes, all right?"

"But I'm not cold. Where are you going?" Billie said. She sounded mildly annoyed.

"No need for you to come back, Donovan," Neil said. "I'll make sure your sister gets home safe."

"Do that, Bennett," Jon said. "Decent hour. No funny business."

"Jon! All right already!" Billie exclaimed and rolled her eyes. "Why don't you go and...and..." She swallowed the rest of what she wanted her brother to go and do and cleared her throat.

Neil smiled at Jenny. "I'll call you, Jenny. I hear you have a daughter and an aunt. I'd like to meet them."

"Tomorrow." Jenny rose to hug him, and Neil wrapped her into his arms. "I'll make sure to prepare them for the visit. And I'd like to meet your son as soon as possible."

"Are you leaving right now?" Billie asked. "Jenny? What about the cheese sandwiches?"

"Later, you two!" Jenny called, stepping into the corridor, and then she and Jon were on the stairs and out of the lighthouse, leaving Billie and Neil alone.

CHAPTER 23

Neil sat in the vacated chair. "Erm. Sorry about that."

Billie crossed her ankles. But it felt weird. She uncrossed them again, wishing she'd worn jeans after all. "Sorry about what?"

He gestured at the door, then ran his hands through his hair. "The excitement, I guess. Your brother suggesting...whatever it was. There was a lot going on."

"You don't have to be sorry for that."

He relaxed lower in his chair, the tension in his shoulder visibly leaving. "I didn't mean to ignore you."

"You didn't. It's all right." Billie tugged on her dress. It wasn't a hot day, but the atmosphere felt oppressive. Maybe it was the fire—or maybe the fact that Jon and Jenny had left the way they did—that made her feel too warm.

"Are you okay?" Neil asked.

"I feel like I need some fresh air," she admitted. "Neil, I think I'll get going too."

He straightened. "We could go up into the beacon room. It's cooler up there."

For a moment, Billie considered. Running away sounded easy. She could be off the island and home in twenty minutes straight, sit in her cottage garden or bake in her kitchen, a cello concerto playing softly on the speaker while she whipped up a fluffy strawberry delight.

"It's all right, Billie." Neil rose. "I'll see you to the door."

"Um." Billie glanced at him from under her lashes but didn't get up.

Neil tilted his head. "There's no reason to be scared of me," he finally said. "Are you? Is that what it is?"

Now she smiled. "Neil, I'm not scared of you. But I have not...dated. Anyone. For a long time. I honestly don't know what to do."

"Same." He smiled back. "I don't know what to do, either."

"No—that can't be true." The words fell from her lips before she could hold them back.

His smile deepened. "No? Are you calling me a liar?"

"I was just—I can't believe you haven't dated anyone for as long as me," Billie hastened to explain. "I raised the boys on my own, you know? I didn't have time to look for a partner or, to be honest, the inclination. And the boys are grown men now."

"You haven't had the inclination to date? At all? You didn't feel like you wanted to share your life with a partner?"

Billie looked down at her hands. "Well...maybe once the boys were more independent, I would have liked to.

But this is a small town." She met his eyes. "There aren't that many men who would date me, and even fewer *I* would date." Billie shrugged awkwardly. Was he going to think she was being extra? Too picky? Unloving? She didn't want him to think any of those things about her.

"I hear you."

She looked up. "Really?"

"Yeah." He stood. "In fact, I've been through something similar. Only for me, it was the traveling, not the small town, that limited the pool of eligible ladies."

"Everyone you met wanted long-term relationships? Really?"

"No, but I did. I'm not a one-and-done kind of guy, if you know what I mean."

Billie blinked. "You have a son," she said disjointedly as she followed her meandering thoughts.

But Neil understood what she wanted to know. "His mom, Inês, left me a long time ago. We're on good terms, but I haven't seen Inês in...maybe fifteen years? She still lives in Portugal. At least, I think she does."

Billie nodded. "I'm sorry."

Neil shook his head to show there was no need. "Nothing to be sorry about. Let's say I was ready to move on a decade ago." His lips moved as if he wanted to say something else, but then he gave a low chuckle. "Listen to us, Billie."

She smiled. "I know."

"Maybe we should have another coffee date before we go into more details of our romantic pasts?" He shrugged a crooked smile at her. "Baby steps?"

"Baby steps." Billie exhaled, relieved. For a moment, it had felt as if they were negotiating the terms of their life together. She liked Neil. Very much. But she barely knew the man. Baby steps were exactly what she needed to make up her mind.

Neil held out a hand. "Wherever we go from here—my feeling is that at the very least, we'll be good friends."

Billie took it and rose. His hand was hard and warm, and his fingers closed over hers. Holding him felt right. "I feel it too," she agreed. "We'll be very good friends."

CHAPTER 24

The sun hovered like the lost golden ball of a fairy-tale princess at the bottom of the sky, ready to roll off the edge and disappear in the ocean while the last evening light danced and glittered over the leaves of the old oaks and young grapes in the vineyard. The long wooden dining tables and benches glowed and gleamed in all the colors of molten bronze and copper, and, wound around the aged wood beams of the open terrace roof, the first string lights twinkled to life.

"Okay." Jenny set down her glass of Jon's best vintage red. "Audrey, Auntie—I have to tell you something."

"It's never good when you call me Auntie," Aunt Georgie said, apprehension dripping from her words. "What now?"

"I never call you Auntie, full stop." Jenny took a deep breath. Beside her, Jon moved, taking her hand that was resting on the bench between them.

Audrey sat up straighter. "What is it, Mom? Are you pregnant?"

A choked sound escaped Aunt Georgie's throat, and Jenny and Jon both laughed, startled.

"No, sweetheart, I'm not. I found out a few things about this family that I want to share." She looked up. "With you in particular, Aunt Georgie."

"Oh no." Aunt Georgie's eyes widened. "Jenny, I only just managed to come back here. Not running away is all I can do right now. Honestly, if it has to do with Mom or my sister, I don't want to know."

Jon's grip tightened, encouraging Jenny. "You *have* to know, Aunt Georgie," she said gently. "I know it sounds fuzzy-wuzzy to your old pirate ears, but you need healing. You need to understand more about what happened so you can move forward."

"No. No. No, I don't need to move forward. I'm almost sixty. I'm happy where I am. I don't want—Did you just call me an old pirate?"

"Fiddlesticks, you are happy." Jenny let go of Jon to take Aunt Georgie's hands in both of hers. "Listen to me. Back then, in the forest?"

Aunt Georgie closed her eyes but left her hands where they were.

"My Mom—Willow—she cut the collar in the car so that Bobby would run. She knew you would go after him."

Slowly, Aunt Georgie's eyes opened. "What?"

"We can't be entirely sure," Jenny added. "But pretty darn sure. Ninety-eight percent, I'd say."

"We?" Audrey looked at Jon. "Who's we? You and Mom?"

He shook his head. "Not in this case."

"By we, I mean Neil and I," Jenny said. "It turns out..." She took another quick breath. "There is a good chance that Neil and I are siblings. Uh, half-siblings. Half-siblings."

The strength left Aunt Georgie's hands. The grip of her fingers loosened. Jenny placed them gently on the table, covering them with hers. "We've ordered a DNA test," she said softly. "I don't have it back yet, but Aunt Georgie—I think I know now who my father is."

The test instructions had said it would take about three weeks for the results to return. Jenny had lain awake at night, wondering whether she should wait for them before telling her aunt about the journal. But by the morning, it had become clear to her that Aunt Georgie didn't need to be coddled.

For once, Jenny wanted her aunt to understand exactly what she was going through. For once, she would make her aunt walk the path with her.

"He was the lighthouse keeper," Aunt Georgie suddenly whispered. "It was always the lighthouse keeper. Ray. Ray Bennett."

Jenny almost flinched with surprise. "You knew?"

"I did not." Now it was Aunt Georgie who leaned forward. "Not until now. You just told me."

Jenny studied her aunt for a moment. Had she known about her sister's love all along? But Aunt Georgie's eyes were open and clear. What just moments ago had seemed to be the beginning of a cataract paling the blue irises was gone. A veil had lifted off her sight, and they were as bright and blue as the Pacific.

"Ray Bennett? Who's that?" Audrey sounded confused.

"He was Neil's dad." Jenny turned to her daughter. "And likely mine. We found an old journal of his. He wrote that it was possible."

"But you don't know?"

"Not a hundred percent. But I'm as sure as I can be without a test."

"Willow wasn't like that!" Aunt Georgie's voice was as hard as a whip.

Jenny stared at her aunt. She'd never heard her speak in that voice.

Aunt Georgie exhaled. "Willow *wasn't* like that," she repeated, softer now. "She didn't sleep around. She was in love with your father. I always envied her that. Stupid and petty as I was, I envied poor Willow, who was in love and had a daughter."

Jenny moistened her lips. She didn't know what to say. She'd never ever for a second thought her aunt envied Willow her status as a single mom. It had always seemed as if Aunt Georgie felt Willow had messed up.

"Hey. Y'all hungry?" Just then, Hannah, face flushed with the heat of the food truck's stove and eyes beaming, arrived at their table. She came with two heavy plates in her hands and two teenage helpers, each carrying a big tray.

"Yes." Jon smiled and stood to take the plates. "Thanks, Hannah, this smells amazing."

"You bet it does," Hannah said, satisfied. "That one's Jenny's. Grilled peach and prosciutto salad with crumbled goat cheese, candied pecans, and a balsamic peach reduction."

"Thank you," Jenny said mechanically and took the beautiful salad.

Hannah glanced at her but didn't say anything. "And this is for Auntie, lemon herb-grilled salmon."

"I'm not your auntie," Aunt Georgie said, sounding just as mechanic as Jenny.

"No, but I wish you were," Hannah said, mild sarcasm in her voice. "What's wrong with you two?"

"Nothing," Jon said charmingly. "Bit of a family discussion. All is well."

Hannah shook her head. "I should say so, sitting here on this wonderful terrace and enjoying"—she checked the next plate—"my delicious orzo pasta tossed with cherry tomatoes, lemon, parmesan, and my secret lemon dressing."

"Do you always have to list every single ingredient?" Aunt Georgie sounded stressed.

"Yes, I do, darling." Hannah was not easily intimidated. "Part of my job description."

"That's mine," Audrey said with an apologetic look for her aunt's rudeness and took her plate. "It looks wonderful, Hannah."

"And last but not least, this is yours, Jon. Herb-grilled steak with chimichurri sauce." Hannah set the remaining plate in front of Jon and placed a hand on his shoulder. "You need a way out of whatever this situation is? You and I could go toss a big old mozzarella salad with balsamic vinaigrette, if you know what I mean."

"I'm going to assume you mean that quite literally," Jon said and laughed. "Thanks for the offer, but I'm going to stay here and eat my steak. I can't wait another moment. It smells too good."

"That's the sort of validation this cook's heart was looking for." Hannah waved her teenage waiters to come back to the truck with her.

"Thank you, Hannah," Jenny called after her. "Sorry! Thank you! Oh shoot. I was a bit late, wasn't I? Now she thinks there's a situation."

Jon chuckled. "Hannah's all right," he said comfortably. "She was just pulling your leg."

Jenny blinked and stabbed an olive with her fork. It tasted good, salty and sweet and acidic all at the same time. "Is it true what you just said, Aunt Georgie?" she asked. "You envied Mom?"

"Until she was gone, obviously." Aunt Georgie shook her head. "Maybe it was because I was the second daughter or because Mom threw herself into the cause of single mothers and Willow got all the attention. And maybe I envied Willow because she had what I wanted and couldn't have."

"You couldn't have what?"

"Love. A child. Believe me—nobody looked at me when Willow was around. She had the sort of wild, untamed beauty men can't resist." Aunt Georgie cleared her throat. "Not that it matters now what I felt. It barely mattered back then."

But Jenny wasn't done yet. "You envied Willow her child? Her daughter? Me?"

Aunt Georgie sighed. "Yes. Yes, Jenny. I did. I wished you were mine so hard it hurt."

Jenny looked at Jon. He frowned.

"Then why—" She turned back. "Then why were you not there for me?"

"What are you talking about?" Aunt Georgie didn't meet her eyes. She'd pressed her hands to her stomach as if she were sick.

"When we went to Nantucket. It didn't seem like you wanted me."

It took Aunt Georgie a while to answer. "I wanted you," she finally whispered. "I always wanted you to be my daughter. I thought..."

Jenny had to lean forward to catch the soft words.

"You should hate me," Aunt Georgie whispered. "Because I left Willow. I left her alone."

"I never hated you. I love you, Aunt Georgie. Whatever you did or didn't do, I've always loved you."

"But why?"

Jenny didn't know how to answer that. "Why not?"

"No, really." Aunt Georgie set down her fork and knife. "I killed your mother. Maybe not with my hands, but with my envy. My selfishness. She didn't enjoy my company. She couldn't confide in me. Had I been a better person, she'd have confided in me like sisters are supposed to. When she died, and I finally had you for myself, I couldn't even take care of you. Every time I looked at you, I saw my sister's eyes look at me, so I failed her again. So why, Jenny? Why on earth would you love me? I failed you and your mother in all the ways. Having played hide-and-seek with you as a child can't make up for that, even for a soul as sweet as yours."

Jenny exhaled. She remembered the long hours of her childhood when her aunt had played with her. And yes—they alone would have been reason enough to keep loving her. But there was so much more Jenny kept in her heart. "I don't need a reason. I love you because I *know* you, Aunt Georgie." Her voice wavered with all that she felt. "I love you because I know the way you sail a boat. I know how you pick huckleberries, and I know how much you love finding sand dollars. I know you laughed at Grandma's jokes even when they weren't good, and you braided Willow's hair to make her beauty shine even more, and you made all our beds every morning so we didn't have to." Jenny swallowed as the images of all that her aunt meant to her flooded back. "I love that your favorite dress was yellow. I know the shape of your feet and the reasons you don't enjoy knitting. I know the sad bits in romance novels make you cry, and I know how very much you loved all your little dogs. I *also* know how very much more you loved your sister. You loved her more than anything."

Aunt Georgie closed her eyes. "I love you more than anything too," she whispered. "But a love like that is dangerous."

Jenny rubbed her hands over her face. She couldn't dispute the fact that love—and loss—could hurt. "Mom knew the risks of going into the forest alone. She took them willingly. She *didn't give you a choice*, Aunt Georgie."

For a while, they all sat silently, looking at each other. Then, Jenny said, "Can Neil come visit us at home tomorrow?"

"My...nephew?" Aunt Georgie said the words slowly as if she had to taste them first.

Jenny nodded and smiled at her daughter. "He would very much like to see you two again."

"Auntie, say yes already. I want to see my new lighthouse uncle asap." Audrey smiled widely. She'd been eating all along but now put down her fork. "Yay! Another family meeting! Right?"

"Yes," Aunt Georgie said weakly. "Tell him to come. And you, child, don't call me Auntie. I'm your great-aunt Georgiana."

"Sure, Auntie." For a moment, Audrey leaned her head on Aunt Georgie's shoulder. "Sure you are, my sweet, scary auntie."

CHAPTER 25

Jenny took a moment to neaten her outfit, smoothing the wrinkles in her skirt and blouse. Then she drew a deep, cleansing breath, blew out her cheeks, and pushed open the hotel's front door. "Welcome, Neil!"

Their eyes met, and a feeling of homecoming washed over her. She beamed up at her potential relative, whose lips curved upward in a gentle arc.

"Hey, Jenny."

"Do you have it?" she said eagerly.

He lifted the sealed envelope. "Didn't even sneak a peek, as promised."

"Ooh." Jenny clasped her hands under her chin. "The final word, huh? It's now or never."

His eyes mirrored the warmth of his smile as he lifted the envelope a little higher out of her reach. "Do you want it to be a yes or a no?"

"I want it to be a yes so bad I feel like I have a fever." Jenny laughed nervously.

Neil put his hand to her forehead, then pulled lightly on a strand of her hair before brushing it behind her ear. "Feels normal." His lips tugged upward into a quiet smile. "You're probably just lying."

"It must be true that we're related." She shook her head at him. "Because you're already behaving like an annoying older brother."

"I do what I can." He handed her the letter from the genetic testing laboratory and peered over her shoulder. "So what, are you going to let me in or nah?"

"Yes." Jenny stepped aside, clutching the precious results. "Come in, Neil."

His nostrils flared slightly, and then he walked into the hotel's lobby, where he stopped to wait for Jenny to close the door. Sunlight streamed through the windows and reflected off the old sea-glass chandelier. "What a beautiful old house this is," Neil murmured. "I've never been here before."

"Did your dad ever come to visit, do you think?" Jenny had wondered in her sleepless hours at night, when she had lain in bed, thinking about her mother, and her aunt, and the love of a young man that had been as steady as the lighthouse that guarded the untamed coast.

Instead of answering, Neil took her chin and tilted her head so their eyes met. "Don't you mean *our* dad?"

Jenny smiled nervously, conscious of the dry, smooth paper envelope in her hands. "Shall we?" Her voice quivered as she spoke because she wanted it to be true so badly. "Audrey and Aunt Georgie are waiting for us outside. Aunt Georgie can barely eat; she's so on edge."

"Let's not keep her waiting any longer, then." He smiled serenely, but Jenny could tell by the narrowing of his eyes that he was nervous too.

She had met him barely a handful of times since she told her little family in the vineyard what they had learned from Ray's journal. But as if she'd known him for years, she already knew how to decipher the slight changes in his tone of voice, the tilt of his eyebrows, and the set of his mouth.

Now, she hooked her arm under his, and together, they walked through the hotel. On the way, Jenny showed him the kitchen and the glass cabinets in the corridor, the dining room and the small parlor and the grand living room with the wall of glass French doors looking out over the cove. He admired them, but just before they stepped outside, Neil extracted himself gently from her arm.

He glanced outside, where Aunt Georgie and Audrey were plainly visible, sitting with their backs to the living room as they watched the sea lion Polly nurse her brand-new baby.

"What is it?" Jenny blinked in confusion.

He pressed his lips together. "Let's not...overwhelm them."

"Walking arm in arm isn't going to overwhelm them," Jenny whispered back. "What are you talking about?"

He shook his head as if she didn't understand.

"What?"

"It's... What if we're not related after all? What if the letter says we were wrong? It'd be a terrible disappointment." He grazed his thumb against his stubbled chin.

Jenny's heart skipped a beat. Not because she was afraid the letter would deny them siblinghood—she had no doubt about it. But it touched her deeply to see how much Neil wanted her to be his sister.

She slipped her arm back through his, her fingers resting on his forearm. "Nonsense," she murmured. "Pull yourself together, man."

"*You* pull yourself together," he murmured back and brought his hand down gently, covering hers. "Let's go already."

"That's what *I* said."

"Pfft. Yeah. Right."

Grinning, together, they stepped out of the house and onto the sun-warmed stone patio. "Hey," Jenny called out a fair warning to her kin.

Audrey swiveled in her chair and jumped up. "Neil! I thought you'd never get here!"

"Hey, Audrey." With a warm, welcoming smile, he went to her to shake hands, but Audrey unabashedly threw her arms around him and squeezed him tightly.

He chuckled and patted her back. "Hey. How is it going there, kid?"

"Excellent, obviously." Audrey let go and stepped back. "So, Neil, are you my uncle, yes or no? I've never had an uncle, so please say yes."

Neil pressed his lips together and took Audrey's hands between his own for a moment. "I've never had a niece," he said. "But I haven't opened the letter yet. I really hope your mom and I got it right, and that letter says what it's supposed to say."

"Hello, Neil." Aunt Georgie hauled herself to her feet with a not-so-subtle clearing of her throat.

With a sunny, ear-to-ear grin, Audrey sat back down.

Neil turned to Aunt Georgie. "Hello." He held out a hand across the table between them, and Aunt Georgie shook it once, her eyes sharp.

The muscles in his jaw clenched nervously. "Miss Summers, I hope you don't...I don't know. Mind."

Aunt Georgie sat back down composedly, but Jenny thought her aunt was a shade paler than before Neil had arrived. "Mind what? What would I mind?" Her voice wavered, but she quickly caught it. "You being Ray Bennett's son?"

"Mind having me..." Neil shook his head.

"Mind having him be part of this family, of course," Jenny helped him out.

Aunt Georgie's face flushed with a rosy hue, betraying her nervousness. She didn't answer the question but said, "Call me Aunt Georgie, darling, one way or the other. My sister was Miss Summers; I never liked being called by my last name."

His laughter lines deepened as he offered a genial smile. "I'd like that—Aunt Georgie."

Jenny smiled her thanks at Aunt Georgie and put a hand on Neil's arm. "Here, sit down. Audrey baked us a cake. Let's have a piece before doing anything else."

"Sounds good." Neil pulled out a chair between Jenny and Aunt Georgie, and they sat.

"Specifically, a dark chocolate truffle cake," Audrey declared cheerfully. "I think it is just the thing to soothe our nerves while we open the letter."

"That is good thinking."

"To be transparent, I have to give Jon credit for the actual recipe, as well as showing me how to make ganache." She lifted the cake cutter and cut pieces so big and hefty they started laughing.

"What are you trying to do to our waistlines?" Jenny lifted her plate to receive the offered slice. She inhaled, catching a waft of bittersweet cocoa, roasted coffee, the sweet, caramelized aroma of brown sugar, and the subtle nuttiness of toasted almonds.

"I thought this would...uh." Audrey tilted her head critically, surveying her handiwork. "It *is* a bit big, isn't it? Do you want me to cut it in half?"

"Don't you dare." Jenny took her fork and quickly pushed the enormous hunk of cake from the cutter onto her plate. "I've had Jon's chocolate cake before. I want every last crumb."

Smiling triumphantly, Audrey filled the other plates while Jenny poured coffee and tea and handed around cream and sugar.

They started eating, and when they were warm and full of sugar and chocolate and cream, the conversation turned to the journal, Ray, and Willow.

"This is the most family thing I've done in decades," Neil remarked after the story of the journal and all speculations had been shared once more. He was barely halfway through his cake but put down his fork. "This is delicious, Audrey. But I think I have to take a break."

Audrey looked up. "Don't you like it?" She sounded crestfallen.

"No, I do. I do. I like it very much. Here, I'm eating it. No break." Neil picked his fork back up, showing it to Audrey as evidence that he was going to continue, and took another bite. After what looked like a brief internal struggle, he lowered the fork again. "I'm, erm, just not used to eating that much cake. I'm not much of a sweet guy."

Jenny smiled. "You don't have to eat it all now," she said and nodded peacefully at her daughter. "Not everyone is used to our portions of tortes and cakes, sweetheart."

"Leave the poor man alone, child," Aunt Georgie ordered. "Maybe he prefers sausage or cheese. Some people do."

"Fine. You can take the rest home then," Audrey said graciously. "But you have to come more often and train whatever cake muscle Mom thinks she's referring to. You ate barely half of it, and even Aunt Georgie is almost done with her entire slice."

"It isn't polite to comment on how much people eat," Aunt Georgie remarked, still chewing. "I didn't realize I was being monitored."

Jenny noted that her aunt looked happy. Her eyes were bright, her forehead had smoothed, her shoulders relaxed.

"I promise to come back soon and train eating more cake. Erm. Thank you," Neil said politely. "Jenny? How do you feel about looking up the status of our related-ness now? I don't think we should wait any longer. I'm getting too used to having a sister and a niece."

"And an aunt," Aunt Georgie said bossily. "I'm still here too."

Neil's eyes crinkled with delight as he flashed a smile. "Yes. If you'll have me as a nephew, Aunt Georgie."

"Nothing much I can do about it, can I? If you are my nephew, then that's that." But Aunt Georgie's smile was one Jenny remembered from her childhood, when her beloved aunt had been whole and happy.

"Right," Neil said. "We'll go along with whatever we get." He leaned back, crossing his arms in front of his chest as if he needed to shield himself from what was coming next.

"It really is time to know for certain, isn't it?" With a beating heart and her cake forked between her lips, Jenny handed him the letter that had lain beside her plate. "Go ahead."

He hesitated, looking at her to make sure she didn't want to be the one reading the letter.

She pulled it back. "Neil?"

"Yes?"

"Whatever this says about you and me—whether we are brother and sister..."

"Yes."

She tilted her head. "I want you to know that either way, you have a place in this family. Our parents loved each other. Whether or not Ray was my actual dad—he said he wanted to be. Genes or not, that's enough for me. That's more than I ever had. As far as I'm concerned, we already are brother or sister. What do you think?"

Neil looked at her for a moment, and then he bowed his head. When he lifted it again, he was smiling, but Jenny thought she saw him blink. "Even if we're not actually related?"

"Yes," Jenny said, and beside her, Audrey repeated the word under her breath. "Deal?"

He nodded. "Deal."

"Here." Jenny handed him the letter and squeezed her eyes shut. "Go ahead."

She heard the paper ripping, and then, nothing.

She opened her eyes again. Neil was frowning at the words. "No?" she whispered, only now realizing how much she'd wanted it to be really, truly true after all. She wanted Ray, the man who'd loved Willow and whom Willow had loved back, to be her father. And she wanted Neil to be her actual, real-life brother.

He let the paper flutter to the table and met her eyes.

"Oh, come *on*!" Audrey grabbed the letter and let out a hearty cough to grab everyone's attention. Then she read out loud.

We are writing to inform you of the results of the genetic analysis that you and another individual underwent at our laboratory. The purpose of this analysis was to determine the likelihood of a familial relationship between the two of you.

"Right." She stopped to take a breath before she continued. "Here it comes."

Based on the comprehensive genetic testing performed, we are pleased to share with you the following information: The genetic analysis indicates a 99.9%

probability that you and Neil Henry Bennett share a direct biological relationship. Specifically, the data obtained from our tests strongly suggests a half-sibling relationship between the two of you. This conclusion is based on a thorough examination of genetic markers, DNA sequences, and allele patterns.

"Oh," Jenny said weakly. A sigh of relief escaped her lips as she exhaled deeply. Neil's eyes still held hers, and his face was more vulnerable than she'd ever seen before. "Yes. We are," she whispered. "We are half-siblings."

Ray was her dad. Ray had been Willow's lover and the father of her child.

"Yes, we are," Neil said softly. "You really are my little sister, Jenny."

Audrey read on, now in a low murmur.

Please note that the probability of a half-sibling relationship is extremely high. Our laboratory follows rigorous quality control measures to ensure the accuracy of these results, and the percentage provided reflects the confidence level in the findings.

She laughed quietly. "Here, last sentence: *We understand that this information might be surprising and may raise questions.*"

Across the table, Aunt Georgie started crying.

CHAPTER 26

Billie looked up, watching her brother push back his chair and stretch. "Neil?" The night was colder than usual, and instead of the vineyard terrace, they were sitting around one of the barrel-tables in the winery's tasting room. Hannah was off visiting family in Oregon, but Michael had manned her food truck and prepared the best spaghetti that Billie had eaten in a long time.

Neil looked up. "Yes?"

"How about we go fishing? I have to get some of the trout out of the stream, and it's as good a time as any."

"Sounds doable." Neil emptied his glass of wine.

"Gabe?" Jon looked at the detective.

Gabe lifted a hand. "Good luck, but it's a pass for me. I'm going to get the ladies home safely. They've had too much to drink to drive themselves."

"Good man." Jon stood, and so did Neil.

Billie absent-mindedly twirled a strand of hair around her finger. She didn't want Neil to leave. But, in a reversal from her earlier feelings about the matter, she now wanted Jon and Neil to be friends. Fishing was a good bonding activity for men.

Neil looked at her with a small, crooked smile, and for a moment, Billie wondered whether he could read her thoughts.

She smiled back, but he turned to talk to Jon about hooks and sinkers. She looked at her hands.

Nothing more had happened between them since the day after the lighthouse dance. They'd agreed on baby steps—and that's exactly how it felt. A word here, a quick smile there. They hadn't even managed another coffee date because Neil had been busy working on the lighthouse, and Billie had finally had another rescue animal—a little female seal she'd named Sandy—to nurse back to health. But Sandy had recovered and been released back into her natural habitat, and still there'd been no call or coffee date. Not even a walk on the bluff. Nothing.

Maybe it was her own doing?

On that last meeting, Neil had led her up into the cool beacon room because she'd felt too warm. They'd sat next to each other in the buttery soft armchairs, talking until the sun had set and the world around them had turned the color of a ripe summer plum.

When he offered to bring her home again, she had lost her nerve after all. He was too handsome, and too nice, and too *everything*. Her life was peaceful. Maybe lonely, especially now that almost all her friends had partners. But peace was good. It was more than enough. She'd chickened out, and instead of letting him bring her home and give him that goodnight kiss, she'd ran off like a...

"Billie?" Jenny put a hand on hers, stopping Billie from picking on the nail that had started to tear in the corner.

When Billie looked up, her brother's eyes rested on her, and a slight frown pulled on his brow. "Let's go, Neil," Jon said briefly and stood.

Jon was never short-tempered. Least of all with her. He probably thought she'd rejected Neil or something.

Billie pressed her lips together and looked away. She was a grown woman in her forties. She didn't need her brother to approve or disapprove of her choice. Including her love life.

Neil stood too. "Bye, everyone." He put a hand on Jenny's shoulder, and she smiled up at him.

"Bye, Neil. See you soon," Jenny said.

"Bye." Billie tapped her foot impatiently. The two were brother and sister, so that was fine.

But Neil was the sort of man who attracted women without trying.

The female tourists in the winery glanced up when he passed their tables on the way out. They changed their posture to sit a little straighter, tossed their hair over their shoulder, or smoothed their dresses.

And that was also fine... He *was* handsome. Middle age looked good on him. He also was the lighthouse keeper on charming Mendocino Island. No woman could help but fantasize a little about sitting by that fireplace, warm and cozy in Neil's arms while the winter wind howled around the old tower...

"Billie?" Faye leaned toward her, a hand on her swelling belly. "Hey. Are you all right?"

Billie blinked. "Of course. I'm all right."

"Okay. Only because...brace yourself." Faye tilted her head back slightly, indicating the tasting room's door behind her.

Billie craned her neck to look past her friend. "Oh. Great." Her ex, Ian, was holding the door for Francesca, who looked lovelier than ever with her long black hair and shining black eyes and really very tight, knitted, off-white dress that suited her better than anything Billie had worn her entire life.

"Right." Faye soothingly patted Billie's shoulder. "I know you're fine, but...more wine?"

Wordlessly, Billie pushed her glass over. Faye refilled it.

Beside her, Gabe positioned himself to block Billie's view of the door. "Is that better?" He smiled at Billie.

Billie nodded, and then she drained her glass. To be fair, she'd already had a couple. But this glass was the one that made the difference. "Hmm," she hummed as her blood vessels relaxed and warmth flooded her limbs. "Yes. That's better."

"Oh, hello!" Jenny picked up the bottle and held it against the light. "That's enough for you, Bills. You aren't much of a drinker."

"She's okay," Faye said consolingly. "You *are* all right, Billie, aren't you?"

"I mean." Billie propped her face into her hands. "I guess."

She saw Faye and Jenny exchange a glance. Luckily, Audrey was engaged in a lively discussion with her great-aunt. At least Billie didn't have to feel guilty about corrupting the very young or very old as she pulled the second bottle on the table closer.

"No, no, no. Give me that." Jenny lifted it out of Billie's grip. "Your brother won't thank you for staggering around his winery."

"Hmpf." Billie scowled. "I can do what I want."

Jenny leaned closer. "So then do it," she whispered. "What is it really? Because it's not getting drunk, my dear."

Faye leaned in from the other side. "All stations on alert. Ian's coming over."

Billie sighed and squared her shoulders, plastering on a smile.

Francesca smiled back and lifted her hand in greeting as the couple passed, then sat on the chair Ian pulled out for her at an empty barrel table. Ian whispered something in her ear and made his way back to them.

"Hi, Billie. Faye. Jenny. Gabriel." His eyes rested for a moment on Audrey and Aunt Georgie, who had stopped talking and were seizing him up, but apparently, they weren't worth the effort to get acquainted.

"What's up, Ian?" Billie asked, hoping to hurry the inevitable conversation along.

"Listen, Billie, do you mind if the two of us step out on the terrace for a moment? I want to talk."

Billie exchanged a look with Faye, who imperceptibly shook her head.

"I don't want to go outside. It's too windy, Ian."

It wasn't a lie. The cool breeze coming in from the ocean had picked up, and most diners had given up holding on to their napkins and glasses and come inside. "Faye and Jenny can hear whatever it is. Go ahead."

Ian discreetly cleared his throat as a prelude to his words. "I got a call from a big network. They want me to direct a new series, and they already ran the pilot. The ratings are through the roof."

Billie nodded, fuzzy on what any of that had to do with her. "Congratulations. Sounds like the next big step for you."

"The thing is... I'll have to be in LA."

"Oh. I see. Just after moving here, too." Billie had read in the newspaper that the house he was looking at had been sold. "What are you going to do?"

"I simply can't say no. It's too much of an opportunity. The thing is..." He glanced over at Francesca, who was studying the menu. "She doesn't want to leave."

"But she's an actress. LA is where it's happening. She doesn't want to leave?"

He sighed. "I'm... She's pregnant. She wants to have the kid here, not in LA."

Billie blinked. "She is pregnant?" Jenny wasn't the only one who suddenly had an unexpected half-sibling. "Did you tell the boys?"

"No. I haven't told anyone." Ian held up his hands in a gesture of resignation. "It wasn't intentional. We only just found out." He glanced at Faye, who raised a cool eyebrow back at him.

Billie's lips parted slightly, but then she closed her mouth again. She still didn't see what this had to do with her. "All right, well, it's still doable. It's not the greatest commute, but you could negotiate flights for a couple of weekends each month."

"Actually, I could have my own helicopter." Ian grinned, looking happier than Billie could remember ever seeing him. "So I could come home now and then. But not every night."

Billie nodded. "Then what's the problem? Surely if you can afford a helicopter, you can also afford to get Francesca help in the house and with the baby if she needs it."

"Sure." Ian lowered his voice. "The problem is that she doesn't know anyone in town, Billie. I don't want her to get lonely."

Billie sat back. So what he was asking her, the ex-wife he'd left when she had had two young kids and needed help the most, was to befriend the new, pregnant wife-to-be. She rubbed her chin. "Does she know you're asking me this?"

"No." He took a deep breath and again glanced over his shoulder. "She has no idea. Please don't tell her."

"I will," Billie said.

Ian cocked his head like a dog who didn't understand. "I will? I will tell, or I won't tell, or..."

Billie shook her head. "I like her. She's nice. I'll make sure to introduce her to a few people in the cove."

Ian nodded but moistened his lips. "Thanks. But listen, Billie. Jenny, Faye—I understand this is a lot, coming from me of all people. But...I really was hoping *you* could be her friends."

The women looked at each other, their faces masks. Then the corners of Jenny's lips lifted, and Faye gave a brief nod.

Billie crossed her arms. "Okay."

"Okay...what?" Ian sounded nervous.

"We talked at the dance, and I think we're a little friendly already," Billie said. "Don't worry your artsy-fartsy head about it too much."

"We can have baby playdates," Faye added. "It'll be fun."

"They're looking for a resident artist at Lizzie May," Jenny said thoughtfully. "I have no idea if actors qualify, but I could easily find out. If not, at least they'd be happy to have her for the university's theater group."

"Oof." Ian sounded relieved. "Thanks, ladies. Thank you. I mean it."

Billie leaned forward. "You really love her, don't you?"

He blinked rapidly. "Yes, Billie. I do. I'm sorry."

"Billie? Is he bothering you?" came a deep voice from behind Billie. Startled, she swiveled around. "Oh! Neil! I thought you were gone already."

"We changed our minds. It's too cold for trout fishing. And..." He gave her one of the crooked smiles she liked so much. "I prefer your company over your brother's."

"Yeah?" Billie's cheeks warmed, the way they did when Neil looked into her eyes like that.

"Yeah." A warm smile spread across his lips, but when he looked at Ian, his jaw muscles hardened. "What's up?"

"Nothing." Ian held up his hands in peace.

"Ian, it's okay. You don't have to apologize to me." Billie leaned around Neil to see her ex, aware of the grins on Faye's and Jenny's faces. Audrey and Aunt Georgie had both propped their elbows on the table and their faces in their hands, watching with interest.

"I don't?"

Billie stood. "Neil, have a seat. I'll need a moment."

Neil grumbled something under his breath but took a seat beside Jenny, who calmingly patted his back.

"Ian, I'm glad you found someone you truly love. Everyone should." Billie held out a hand. Ian looked suspicious but took it, and Billie continued. "You truly hurt me. On the good side, you forced me to admit that I made a bad choice. I don't love you, either." She smiled. "I'm sure we both had a better life for not walking that last long stretch together."

Ian looked like he had bit into a sour apple but didn't draw his hand from hers. "At least you're frank."

"I don't like you very much, but I do like your fiancée," Billie said. "I won't lie and say we'll be *best-best* friends—mostly because you will never not annoy me when you are around. But I think Francesca and I can do better than friends. I think we will be good friends."

"Erm."

"You should take what she offers." Neil leaned over to look at Ian.

"Hush." Jenny lightly slapped her brother's arm. "Billie's taking care of it."

"And the two of us...we'll keep playing nice with each other," Billie said. "We have the boys. It'll be easier for them, now that you live here."

Ian started to shake his head, but then he freed his hand from Billie's and pulled her into a hug. "Sounds good, all of it," he murmured into her ear. "I don't love you either, but I really do like you. You have finally forgiven me my sins, haven't you?"

Billie nodded. "Thoroughly. In fact, I never think about you anymore."

"I'm glad." She could feel his smile in his embrace. "I never think about you either. You're a great girl, Billie."

Now it was she who freed herself. "I'm a woman, Ian, not a girl. Tell Francesca hi from us. Also tell her Faye, Jenny, and I are going to meet for coffee and pie at the students market in Maytown on Saturday. Has she been to Maytown yet?"

"I don't think so." Ian's eyes had lost their guarded look, and his face wore the boyish look she used to adore. Not anymore. Now, Billie preferred a man who looked like a man, not a boy.

"Francesca can drive with me, if she meets me at the cottage around nine," Billie offered. "I'll show her how to get there and where to park."

"And while she's on campus anyway, she might as well check out Lizzie May's theater company," Jenny added. "They'll have a stand at the market, and they'll be happy to meet her."

Ian smiled. "Francesca loves performing on the stage. Thank you."

"Tell her to let me know if she needs a good doctor," Faye offered. "I can probably talk the office into taking on a new patient."

"Thank you, that's very kind of you. We will need a new doctor."

Faye nodded, and they all turned to look at Francesca. As if she felt their gazes, the woman turned as well, looking startled to see so many eyes on her.

Billie smiled and made the universal thumb-and-little finger sign for a phone call. Francesca's lips curved upward, and she echoed the gesture back just before a server arrived at the table with a tray and distracted her.

"Go, Ian. She's alone, and your drinks just arrived," Jenny said. "Don't let her sit by herself."

Ian nodded. "Right. Well...I'll see you around." He turned and left.

"Don't call us, we'll call you," Faye muttered, and Billie and Jenny grinned.

Neil pushed his chair back with a slight scrape against the floor, rose, and straightened his shoulders. "Billie?"

She turned to him. "Yes?"

With a tentative smile, he extended his hand toward her, an unspoken invitation for her to join him. His eyes held her gaze as he softly said, "Can we talk for a moment too?"

Behind him, both Jenny and Faye made shooing gestures, telling Billie to go.

She smiled at the lighthouse keeper and put her hand in his, feeling his fingers send sparks of electricity up her arm. "The terrace is beautiful right now."

The curve of his lips deepened into a heartwarming, genuine smile. "Not as beautiful as you are," he murmured.

Jenny and Faye pretended to swoon silently, but Billie ignored them and followed Neil past the crowded tables to the quiet, moonlit terrace.

CHAPTER 27

The night wind that earlier had brought in cool air from the northwest had died down. All that was left now was a sweet breeze that played in the vineyard, here and there rustling through luscious clusters of ripe berries or mischievously lifting lobed leaves to peek underneath. It was too late for new guests, and the ones that had already arrived had comfortably settled inside, enjoying their meals and the rustic ambiance of the tasting room.

Only one other couple stood on the far end of the terrace, their arms entwined in a loving embrace, their lips kissing, their minds oblivious to the rest of the world.

Neil glanced at them, then smiled and leaned against the cast iron railing.

"Why didn't you call me? I waited for you to get in touch."

She bit her lip. "I wanted you to call me. I waited for you to get in touch."

He crossed his arms and raised his face to the night sky so she could no longer see his eyes. "Does your ex want to talk often?"

"Luckily, no. We don't talk often."

He cast a guarded glance at her from beneath lowered lids. "So you two are all done with each other."

"You knew that already, and you heard what I told him just now." She smiled. "Why?"

"I thought, maybe..." He shook his head. "I thought maybe you didn't call me because you were still sorting things out with him after all. It was the only thing I could come up with. Maybe you weren't ready to trust me—or your heart."

"Maybe," she said. "Maybe I still had to fix the last of the damage I allowed him to do to my heart. But all that is over now."

"I'm not a jealous guy, Billie. At least I wasn't until now." His eyes crinkled at the corners.

She took a step closer, close enough to feel the warmth radiating from his body. She no longer felt shy or conflicted about what she was willing to give or receive. Instead, a playful smile appeared on her lips. "No?"

He reached for her, putting his hands on her waist in a way that made her heart drum faster, and pulled her to him. "Like I said, not until now." He tightened his hold even more; she had to tilt her head back to see his eyes. "But you?" he murmured, his eyes studying her face as if committing every detail to memory. "I'm done waiting for another man to come along and ask you for a word on the terrace. You belong to me."

"I see. No more Mr. Nice Guy?"

Billie nestled closer, feeling his body react. "I'm not so good at sharing either," she whispered. "In fact, I'm strictly no-sharing. How do you feel about that?"

"I feel better about that than most other things in my life." His lips met her forehead, and he pressed a kiss on it. "Hey."

Her heart fluttering with a mixture of vulnerability and desire, Billie looked up. Their eyes locked, and she smiled. "Hey," she whispered.

"I know that a few days ago, I said we'd take baby steps," Neil murmured. He loosened his hold to tuck a stray curl behind her ear, letting his fingers trail down her jaw. "But that was then. That is also over. It doesn't work for me after all."

"A handful of days and baby steps are already in the past?" Billie tilted her head back further to see him better. The moon was hiding behind a cloud, but the glow of string lights was enough to see the longing in his eyes.

He lowered his head closer to hers, his gaze burning her lips. "Very much in the past."

"What do we do instead of...of baby steps?" Billie whispered. It was hard to breathe when his mouth was so close to hers.

"Hmm." Neil lowered his head again, his breath brushing her, his lips barely hovering above hers, their heat already warming Billie's own. A small sound escaped her, and when he pulled her even closer, it closed the gap between their lips, so they just touched each other. It was not yet a kiss, but no longer something else, either. "We do this," he murmured, his mouth moving against hers to say the words.

"I don't understand," she whispered, too distracted by the beating of her heart and the feel of his soft, supple mouth to process his meaning. "Like what?"

"Like this." He pressed his lips hungrily down on hers, kissing her fully.

Billie couldn't respond. She wanted to, but it felt overwhelming. This wasn't just a kiss. It was a promise, and a question, and most of all, a beginning.

Neil pulled back, gazing at her with a fierce intensity. "I'm done waiting for you to make up your mind and call me. I want to take the plunge, Billie. I'm all in. I'm all yours. You have the kindest, most beautiful heart and soul I've ever come across, and I'm not going to let you go. Tell me how I can convince you."

Billie's breath caught. "You...are already doing a good job. But go ahead. Convince me some more."

Ian had taught her to be cautious, afraid of making mistakes and getting hurt. But with Neil, she was finally safe. With him, she could be daring.

Billie put her arms around his neck, buried her fingers in his hair, and then she kissed him, leaving no doubt about the intensity of her feelings for him. She, too, was done waiting.

When she finally broke away for breath, Neil groaned. "Don't," he murmured. "Don't stop."

"Let's go home," she whispered.

The other couple had vanished, and they were alone on the terrace. The moon had broken through the clouds once more, dipping the landscape in silver and gold. It was only a matter of time before the door would open and someone would step out to enjoy their dessert under the starry sky.

"Where's home?" Neil ran his hands through his hair and deeply inhaled the clean, warm air. "The cove or the island?"

"The cove." Billie raised on tiptoes and kissed his chin. "My cottage is closer," she whispered.

"Really? Are you sure?"

Billie nodded, rubbing her arms as the cool breeze returned. "I'm sure."

Neil took off his jacket and put it around her shoulders. Instead of going back inside to pick up Billie's purse, they took the stairs off the terrace and walked arm in arm through the moonlit vineyard toward the parking lot. There, Neil stopped.

"I want to take you to the lighthouse," he said in a low voice. "I know your cottage is closer, but let's go to the lighthouse anyway."

She smiled. "Because...why?"

He took the keys from her and unlocked the passenger door of his car, holding it open for her. "Because too many people have a key to your house," he murmured when she climbed in. "And not a soul can come into my place if I don't invite them in."

Billie took a steadying breath that did nothing to calm the butterflies dancing in her belly as she climbed into his car. "I see."

He leaned down so he could see her face. "Too much too soon?"

She reached out and let her hand run along his jaw, feeling the rough stubble. "No," she replied simply, but her fingers trembled.

Smiling, Neil took her hand and kissed them, then closed the door. He got into the driver's seat and started the engine.

The car was warm inside, but the cool breeze blew in through the open windows as they drove along the starry, winding roads through the hills of the vineyard. They stayed in the car as the ferry glided over the glittering water instead of joining the other passengers, lost in each other's presence. When Neil drove off the ferry and turned onto the lane leading to the lighthouse, the last clouds had been blown from the crystalline night sky, and a myriad of stars twinkled over the lighthouse.

When they reached it, Neil parked the car, opened Billie's door, and helped her out. "Thanks." She smiled, realizing she had waited with bated breath for his touch—it was as if she could no longer bear not to touch him.

"You're welcome, my dear." The way he said her name, low and tender, made her breath catch in her throat. He took the jacket she'd left in the car and slung it over his arm, then took her hand. Slowly, they ambled through the winding path and the wild garden toward the lighthouse, where Neil unlocked the door and pushed it open. Once inside, he tossed the jacket onto a chair and came to her.

"Neil?"

He stopped. "Hm?"

She inhaled. "Just...it's been a while."

Wordlessly, he closed the distance between them and picked her up in his arms.

"Don't." Billie wanted to laugh, but she couldn't. "I'm way too heavy. I can walk."

He didn't deign to reply, carrying her up the stairs, past the cozy living room, all the way to the top of the lighthouse, as if she weren't a curvy woman in her forties with a fondness for baking, only stopping once they got to the beacon room.

Neil kicked open the door and stepped inside with Billie still in his arms, then he kicked it shut behind them. "I've wanted to carry you up here since the first time I laid eyes on you." He lowered her onto her feet, and his lips curved into a quiet smile. "But if you leave, I'm not going to come after you."

"I'm not leaving." Billie smiled and walked deeper into the room, to the largest window looking out to the sea. The thick wall was made out of brick and stone, and it was cool against her shoulder as she leaned against it to gaze out. Neil came to stand beside her.

"I want to remember this moment forever," he said softly. "You, standing here, in the moonlight." He took a breath. "You're so beautiful, Billie."

"It's not just my heart you like?" She gave him a playful look.

"You are beautiful inside and out. Maybe this is a good time for a fair warning." He reached out, slipping his hand beneath her curls, and tenderly cradled her head.

Billie leaned into his hand. "What sort of warning?" she whispered.

"I won't be able to keep my hands off you." His voice was barely a murmur. "I managed so far, but that's the third thing this evening that is over now."

"I don't want you to." Billie bit her lip, her heart hammering in her chest. "I want you to love me."

"Good." Neil pulled her in until his mouth met hers. He kissed her deeply, his hand caressing her shoulders and roaming down, until she couldn't help but cry out a sound that was new to her throat and lips but old as the sea herself. Billie's back arched, and she closed her eyes and let go, giving herself over to feelings and sensations she had never, in all the years of her marriage, known before.

CHAPTER 28

The cool, northwestern front had long left Mendocino Cove again. The afternoon was hot, but the umbrella provided shade, and a pleasant sea breeze cooled them just enough to be outside. Carefully, Jenny set Christy's filled coffee cup on the patio table. "Here you go," she said. "As hot and black and sweet as a summer night, the way you like it. Help yourself to cake and cookies."

"Thank you, Jenny." Christy, every inch a lady with her eggshell silk blouse, gray pencil skirt, gray coiffure, and Parisian-red lips, daintily selected a pink macaron.

"Of course."

Jenny sat back down beside Jon, who smiled reassuringly and took her hand under the table. Jenny let out a quiet breath of gratitude for her man and squeezed his fingers to thank him.

The two of them had already had coffee earlier, sitting on a driftwood log on the beach after they'd gone swimming and enjoying the serene peace of the forgotten cove before their family and guests gathered.

Audrey and Aunt Georgie had been out on a walk across the bluff to pick wildflower bouquets for the living room—and squabble over what vases to use—and were now visibly enjoying the large, milky-white café lattes Audrey had hooked her great-aunt on.

Agatha Simon, Christy's best friend, had played chauffeur to be in on the action and was now cutting into her latest lemon cake experiment.

Across the table, Audrey's widening grin told Jenny that it was time to pull herself back to the moment. She let go of Jon's hand, squared her shoulders, and smoothed her linen dress.

Just when she was about to speak, Agatha set a slice of lemon cake on her plate. "There you go, dearie."

"Thank you, Agatha." Jenny smiled. "It looks excellent. And *very* yellow."

"I *know*," Agatha said happily. "It's that new food coloring I found online. It tastes a bit off, but it's barely noticeable after the almond extract goes in the batter. And the color is simply next level."

"Yes. Great. Um." Jenny stifled a laugh and delicately cleared her throat. "Well—I understand you have news for me, Christy."

The older lady nodded and pushed her sunglasses into her hair. "I apologize it has taken me this long, Jenny." She took a bite of her pastel-colored treat. "But I have good news. At least I think it is good news."

"Great." Jenny smiled. Christy had taken the treasures from the heirloom cabinet to be appraised in San Francisco. There had been a couple of delays and waiting periods, but the right people had finally returned from an international trip and given Christy estimates for the items.

Christy popped the rest of her cookie into her mouth, brushed a non-existent crumb off her manicured fingertips, and pulled a folded piece of cream-colored paper from her vintage Chanel bag. "Here is the breakdown. Each item is listed with the appraisal beside it, and I summed it up at the end of the column. You understand, naturally, that these are only our best estimates for what you would get at auction."

"Yes, of course." Jenny reached for the paper. Whatever sum would be on there—it was going to be much more than she had in the bank. Her adjunct professor's salary barely paid for groceries and utilities and taxes.

Luckily, Aunt Georgie had not brought up selling the hotel again. A few days ago, Jenny had also submitted her application for the tenure professorship, which was well paid.

But it was very possible that the search committee hired another candidate. No matter for what outcome the head of the department wished, the committee would unerringly pick the most qualified applicant. And Jenny had no idea who all had applied to the position of history professor.

Likewise, it was still possible that Aunt Georgie was going to sell the old family hotel. The last time Jenny had asked about her decision, Aunt Georgie hemmed and hawed and scuttled out of the room as soon as she could. Since no one knew how much money Georgie actually had in the bank, maybe she needed the money from the sale after all.

Jenny looked at the folded sheet of paper, bracing herself.

Of course, her friends would be there for Jenny and Audrey if all else failed. But the last thing Jenny wanted to do was impose on them.

"Go on, Mom. Have a look." Audrey had politely nibbled on a corner of her cake but now put her fork down. Her eyes were wide and worried.

"Yes, sweetheart." Holding her breath, her heart hammering, Jenny unfolded the paper.

Jon leaned over to read over her shoulder. He laughed quietly.

It was... Confused, Jenny looked up. "What? For real?"

Satisfied with her reaction, Christy laughed. "Good?"

Jenny was almost too stunned to speak. "Yes. Yes, very good," she managed.

"Mom?" Audrey held out her hand. With shaking fingers, Jenny put the paper into it. Audrey's eyes flew down the column to the sum total of the estimate. Her mouth opened. "Whoa!"

"Let me see," Aunt Georgie said and took the paper from her great-niece. Her mouth curved into a knowing, conspiratorial smile, and she cleared her throat with a soft cough before she looked up. "Maybe I should have kept that armoire for myself after all, huh?"

Jenny smiled and folded her hands. Her heartbeat hadn't slowed down; instead, the flutter seemed to pick up speed. "Aunt Georgie?"

"Yes?" Aunt Georgie folded the paper and set it on the table, weighing it down with a glass of strawberry lemonade.

"Would you accept the sum on the paper—or rather, the sum the heirlooms will actually bring in at auction—for the hotel?" The estimate on the piece of paper was eye-wateringly high, but still a lowball offer. The huge, historic mansion and the charming cove were worth more.

Aunt Georgie fell back in her chair. "Sell you the hotel?"

"Yes." Jenny blinked nervously.

The money from the auctions was all she and Audrey would have going forward. Buying any house was a financial gamble, let alone one as old as their historic mansion. But they couldn't lose the majestic house. Not only was it their home, but reopening the hotel was the only way Audrey could afford to stay in Mendocino Cove.

And more than the old hotel, Jenny wanted to keep her daughter close.

CHAPTER 29

"If I sell *you* the hotel, where will *I* stay?" Aunt Georgie asked, her voice too casual.

Jenny exchanged a look with Audrey.

Aunt Georgie had not told either of them about her plans for the future. After finally overcoming her deep-seated fear of the place that reminded her so much of the sister she lost, Aunt Georgie seemed to have gotten more and more comfortable. But neither Audrey nor Jenny had thought that Aunt Georgie might stay in Mendocino Cove.

Now, Jenny leaned forward and put a hand on her aunt's. "You want to stay here?" she asked softly.

Aunt Georgie weaved her head. "Maybe for now," she said, being as vague as she could possibly be.

"But, Auntie." Audrey leaned forward with an impish smile. "If Mom and I move out, and you stay all alone in this big place—who is going to make your breakfast so it is ready when you wake up? Who is going to bring your reading glasses from upstairs when you're comfortably settled on the patio? Who remembers which one of your soaps is on which TV channel and who is going to tie eucalyptus to your showerhead?" She blinked innocently. "Who is going to make your café lattes and put a little smiley face in your milk foam?"

"I will, of course. I'm not even sixty," Aunt Georgie said, indignant. "You think I can't run up and down the stairs as often as I like?"

Audrey smiled serenely. "The question is...do you *want* to? No. Of course you don't, or you would. Come on. Sell Mom the house, Auntie."

"Don't call me Auntie, child."

Audrey leaned back and crossed her arms over her chest. "Don't call me child, Auntie."

Jenny patted her aunt's hand. "Of course you'd stay here, my dear. As long as you want to. With us, Audrey and me. We would love nothing more than to have you live with us for good."

Audrey frowned, clearly frustrated. "You're so weird, Auntie; I never know what you'll say next. I love you and want to drink lattes with you forever. One way or the other, don't go back to your cruises. Please?"

"*I'm* weird?" Aunt Georgie raised her eyebrows at Jenny. "Did your daughter just tell me that *I* am weird?"

"Audrey." Jenny smiled at her exuberant daughter. "Aunt Georgie, don't listen to her. You're a little strange. But definitely not weird."

Aunt Georgie shook her head, and then she drained her latte. "Fred also used to say I was a little strange, but he, too, was incorrect." She sighed and looked up, blinking into the azure sky. "You two don't have to worry about the hotel any longer. I've resigned myself to the fact that selling it won't change the past, or make the present any more bearable, or, indeed, change the future. Your company, however, does."

Audrey heaved a huge sigh of relief and closed her eyes. Then she leaned over and rested her head against her aunt's shoulder. "Oh! Thank you. You do have a heart after all! You *do* love us."

Aunt Georgie looked pained, but then she put an arm around her great-niece's shoulders. "I do have a heart, but we don't need to run around *saying* stuff like this all the time, child."

"I love you too." Audrey patted Aunt Georgie's hand on her shoulder. "Come on. Let's say it all the time from now on. I love you, my little old auntie."

Aunt Georgie, with a small snort of impatience, lifted her arm and shrugged her shoulder. "Sit up straight, child. Don't call me Auntie. Eat your cake. Where are your manners? Agatha *labored* over this." She pointed at the cake.

"I don't *labor*, Georgie," Agatha remarked mildly from across the table. "It's called baking. You should try it sometime. Maybe poppyseed cake could be your thing."

"Poppyseeds forever get stuck between the teeth. It's not a very good cake to make one's thing."

"Goodness. What are you...what are we even talking about?" Bewildered, Christy looked, eyebrows raised, from one to the other.

Grinning, Audrey started eating her cake.

Jenny couldn't help but smile at the odd pair in front of her. Audrey had been so apprehensive about her great-aunt—and now, Auntie Georgie seemed to be her favorite person in the cove.

Jenny tapped a finger on the table. "Um. Aunt Georgie?"

"Yes?"

"Can I just... I understand you won't sell the hotel to anyone? Are you sure?"

Aunt Georgie, maybe softened up by her great-niece, smiled. "I'm sure."

"That's great." Jenny put a hand to her temple. Could it be this easy? She tilted her head. "For real? You won't change your mind again?"

Agatha and Christy smiled into their coffee, but Aunt Georgie nodded. "You'll have to put up with me. And fresh eucalyptus on my shower head is nonnegotiable."

"I'm sure that's no problem."

Audrey ate the last bite of her slice of cake. "This is delicious, Mrs. Simon," she declared.

"I know!" Agatha replied happily.

"All is well," Jon murmured and put a hand on Jenny's arm. "I knew your hotel was too beautiful to lose."

"It's not mine," Jenny said reflexively. "It's my aunt's."

"Well, actually," Aunt Georgie chimed in, "it's sort of yours."

Jenny's eyes widened. "Mine?"

"Well..." Aunt Georgie coughed, sounding embarrassed. "It was to be your birthday present. You know—to make up for all the presents I missed giving you over the years." She took a breath. "Darling, clearly I wasn't the aunt I should have been. Since you seem to want this place so badly, I thought...I thought it would help make up for not taking care of you in Nantucket, when you needed me. Or later."

A hush fell over the patio.

"Aunt Georgie—I am... First of all, *thank you*." Jenny's thoughts swirled in her head. "Second, you don't have to make up for anything."

"Yes, I do. I let my sister down in more than one way."

"Stop." Jenny reached for her aunt's hands on the table, taking them in her own. "You have to stop blaming yourself right now. My mother made sure you turned back. She wanted to go off the trail to meet my father. But she couldn't find the path she used to take and lost her way. Maybe she was bitten by a snake when she rested under the root, or maybe she wandered in circles, always just missing the search party. It has happened before to hikers, and it will happen again. It was a terrible accident. But it was not your fault. In fact, your sister played you a little dirty. You could have lost your dog, or you could have lost direction yourself looking for him. I'm sure she meant no harm. But she had no business playing the odds the way she did."

Aunt Georgie blinked. "I wish I would have let the dog go, not her."

"She *wanted* to go," Jenny said gently. "She was your older sister. She would have found a way. She could have found a better way to meet up with Ray."

Agatha leaned forward. "Georgie, my dear old friend. I wasn't going to say anything, but do you *remember* Willow? Do you *really* remember your sister?"

A tear rolled down Aunt Georgie's cheek. Mute, she nodded.

"Because I knew her very well," Agatha said. "I was older, and I saw her grow up. She was different from the other girls in the cove. Strong, and gorgeous, and wild. Like the forest itself."

Again, Aunt Georgie nodded.

Agatha's face softened. "Never *ever*, on earth or in heaven, would your sister blame you for one moment. Not if it had been your innocent mistake that caused this, even less since she sent you after the dog. I mean, goodness. She *cut* Bobbie's collar, Georgie. What grown woman does that?"

Slowly, Aunt Georgie took a breath.

"It sounds, my dear," Christy said quietly, "as if you have Jenny's permission to let it go. All of it. Isn't that right?" She looked at Jenny.

"Yes. Yes, of course. I want nothing more, Aunt Georgie. Just lay down that burden. It isn't real. There is nothing more for you to carry."

"There is nothing more to carry," Aunt Georgie whispered and exhaled.

And then, something happened.

A shift of energy trembled through Aunt Georgie, rearranging her. She suddenly looked different. Brighter, livelier, younger, as if something large and dark had left like a raptor that no longer needed to roost. "It's gone," she said, sounding surprised.

"It's gone?" Jenny asked, stunned at the transformation.

"I was angry at Willow. She should have stayed on the trail. She should have finished the walk and been at the car."

"Yes, she should have. She knew that too. I'm sure she knew that and worried about you."

"She worried about me..." Georgie repeated, again sounding surprised. "Yes, she would have worried about what she'd done to me, wouldn't she?"

"I guarantee it," Agatha chimed in. "She did what she wanted—but she loved her family dearly. She would have worried about you all once she realized she wouldn't find her way back."

"An accident." Jenny squeezed her aunt's hands. "A terrible accident."

"Yes." Aunt Georgie smiled. It was a sad smile; she would always be sad to have lost her sister. But it was a smile, nevertheless. "Yes, a terrible accident."

"We'll visit her grave, okay?" Jenny said gently. "You and me. So she can see how well we're doing. She'll like that, wherever she is."

"We'll bring her flowers." Aunt Georgie pulled her hands out of Jenny's and pulled a surprised Audrey into her arms. "And you'll come too, darling. We'll all go together."

Smiling, Audrey hugged her aunt back.

"And then..." It was as if the floodgates had opened, and Aunt Georgie couldn't stop talking. Her voice was new, higher and sweeter. "Darling child, you get the hotel ready to open again. We'll offer reduced rates to single mothers, just like Mom did. Maybe the single mothers don't need us anymore. Then again, maybe they do. We'll do it in honor of Willow—and Jenny."

"Yes! Yes!" Audrey jumped up and raised triumphant arms to the sky. "Yes!"

"Yes," Jenny whispered too, but it was drowned out by Audrey's chatter and Aunt Georgie asking Agatha about Willow, and Christy venting her doubt about the too-yellow cake.

"Are you happy?" Jon took Jenny's hand.

CHAPTER 30

J on smiled. "The hotel is finally yours."

"More like hers." Smiling, Jenny nodded at her exuberant daughter, who was detailing all she wanted to do in a waterfall of words and gestures.

He nodded, watching Audrey fondly. "Yes, if the hotel opens again, she'll be the one running it. You'll have enough to do with the professorship."

"I don't know if I'll get that."

"There's a good chance. They told you how much they need your area of expertise. They invited you to apply."

"They did." Jenny couldn't deny that the encouragement she'd received meant she was one of the favored candidates.

"Come to the beach with me," Jon said and rose. "I need a moment of quiet."

Jenny stood, smiling at her noisy family and friends. "We'll be back in a moment. Don't go anywhere."

Arm in arm, she and Jon went down to the water, where they stepped out of their tennis shoes and let the cold waves wash over their feet.

Jon took her into his arms. "I've been meaning to ask for a while now," he said, holding her gaze.

Jenny couldn't help but smile, her heart full of love. "Ask me what?"

"Ask you to marry me," he said. "I know you've been through a lot and said you didn't want to marry again. Even if you wanted to, I realize it might be too soon to ask. But..."

Jenny's breath hitched in her throat. "But what?" she whispered.

"But I have to ask for myself, my love," he murmured. "I *want* to ask you. I want to hear your answer, and I want it to come from your lips, not my imagination."

Warmth spread through Jenny. She hadn't thought about marriage. She was happy the way things were. She couldn't think.

"And should you say yes..." Jon let Jenny go so he could take her hands into both of his. "Then I'll ask whether you will move in with me."

"Into the apartment over the tasting room?"

Smiling, he shook his head. "I met with a friend last month. He's an architect."

"An architect?"

"The winery is doing well, and it's time for me to build a house. Remember how I purchased more land next to the vineyard?"

"Yes—I thought you meant to plant more grapevines."

"That was only until I could build a house. I didn't know the winery would do as well as it does, but there's no reason to wait any longer." He lifted her hands and kissed her palms. "If you say yes, you and I will build our dream house in the vineyard near the oak grove. Or"—he leaned in and lightly kissed her lips—"say no, and we'll still do it."

"Jon..."

"Hmm." Jon let go of her hands and reached into the pocket of his jeans, pulling out a small black velvet box. "I'd go down on my knee, my dear, but we're in the water."

"I don't want you to kneel," Jenny said quickly.

Jon smiled and opened the box.

Jenny stared at the sparkling ring. "Are you serious?"

"Jenny Summers, you are the love of my life. I want you to marry me. I've never been happier than when I'm with you, and I want to make you as happy as you make me. Marry me, my love."

"I have kids...and an aunt." The nervous words came out of nowhere.

Jon's smile deepened. "I'm well aware, love. They're wonderful people, and I'd be honored to make them my family. However, they'll stay here. But you—you'll come with me."

"To the vineyard?"

"Yes, honey." Now, Jon had to chuckle. "You come with me to our vineyard, where we will live in the house we'll build. You will probably be a professor, I'll be a vintner, and in the evenings, we'll eat dinner on the terrace with all our friends and family. Or maybe not. Maybe we'll have dinner alone, at home, or in our favorite secret little spot in the oak grove, or we close the tasting room and have it there." He took a shallow breath. "Jenny—what do you think? I need to hear it from your own lips."

"I think...I think I love you, Jon," Jenny whispered, her voice trembling. "It sounds lovely."

"Yes to the house?"

"Yes to the house."

He put a finger under her chin and lifted her face to his. "Yes to me?"

Jenny smiled as her confusion lifted as sudden as a threadbare morning fog when the sun comes out. "Yes to you, Jon. It was always yes to you."

"You'll marry me," he confirmed.

"Yes, of course I'll marry you."

"Good." He tilted his head as if he couldn't quite believe her. "Just making sure, because you once said you never wanted to marry again."

"I didn't know how much I loved you and enjoyed being with you." Jenny held out her hand and wiggled her fingers. "Ring, please!"

"Ah." He laughed and took the ring off the pillow, then slid it onto her hand. "It was my grandmother's," he murmured, lingering over the task.

"I recognize it," Jenny said sweetly. "I remember seeing it on her finger."

Jon and Billie's grandmother had been one of the best people Jenny had ever known; it was an honor to wear her ring.

Her new ring heavy on her finger, Jenny rose on tiptoes, slipped her arms over his shoulders, and kissed Jon.

"You are the best man in the whole wide world," she whispered. "I'm so very grateful to have you."

"Not as grateful as I am for you," he murmured and kissed her back a little longer than was good for her heartbeat. "We'll walk the rest of this journey hand in hand, my love. Trust me to never let go."

"Yes." Tears of happiness rose in Jenny's eyes. "The rest, we'll walk together." She sank back on her heels to rub her hand over her eyes. "Oh, Jon." She couldn't help but laugh under her tears. "Look at them."

Jon loosened his hold on her to turn to the patio.

Audrey, Agatha, Christy, and Aunt Georgie were staring at them, the older ladies' eyes wide and mouths open.

Slowly, Audrey rose and cupped her hands to her mouth to make a megaphone. "Did you finally ask her, Jon?"

"She said yes! We're getting married!" he called back and waved, and Jenny saw her daughter throw him two thumbs up and clasp her hands delightedly.

"Mom? Is it true?"

Jenny laughed, happier than ever before. "Yes, it's true!"

"Well, well, well!" Aunt Georgie stood with a satisfied expression and opened her arms. "I suppose it's time for a Mendocino Cove wedding!"

Thank you for reading A Lighthouse of Ocean and Fog! *Read the next book in the series,* A Wedding of Hearts and Tides, *to stay in beautiful Mendocino Cove and continue the saga!*

BEACH COVE SERIES

★★★★★ *"What an awesome series! Captivated in the first sentence! Beautiful writing!"*

Maisie returns to charming Beach Cove and meets a heartwarming cast of old friends and new neighbors. The beaches are sandy and inviting, the sea is bluer than it should be, and the small town is brimming with big secrets. Together, Maisie and her sisters of the heart take turns helping each other through trials, mysteries, and matters of the heart. Get the free prequel to the series!

Read the Beach Cove Series

BAY HARBOR BEACH SERIES

★★★★★ *"Wonderfully written story. Rumors abound in this tale of loves and secrets."*

Lose yourself in this riveting feel-good saga of old secrets and new beginnings. Best friends support each other through life's ups and downs and matters of the heart as they boil salt water taffy, browse quaint stores for swimsuits, and sample pies at the Beach Bistro!

MENDOCINO COVE SERIES

★★★★★ *"I loved it all, the history, the mystery, the sea, the love of family and friends...!"*

A gorgeous feel-good series with wonderful characters! Four friends are taking a second chance on love and life as they start over together in the small town of Mendocino Cove. Set on the breathtakingly beautiful coast of Northern California, where the golden hills are covered in wildflowers, vineyards grow sweet grapes, and the coast is rugged and wild.

Read the Mendocino Cove Series

ABOUT THE AUTHOR

Nellie Brooks writes feel-good friendship fiction for women. In her books you'll find flawed, likable characters who bake and adopt animals, gorgeous coastal settings that will make you study your tea leaves for the next vacation date, secrets that are best solved together, and happy endings until every estranged friend and distant sister is safe in the arms of her small town community.

Visit www.nelliebrooks.com to subscribe to her newsletter and hear about releases, promos, and writing news! You can also follow Nellie on Facebook and BookBub.

Made in the USA
Las Vegas, NV
20 February 2024

86042840R00163